DESTINATION DIEPPE

W. Howard Baker

Was it an act of criminal folly? Were
the brasshats hideously wrong? Or was
it a risk, justified in calculation, that
made possible the ultimate victory of
D Day

DESTINATION DIEPPE

W. HOWARD BAKER

ZENITH PUBLICATIONS

Published by Zenith Publications – London

Printed by Hunt Barnard, Aylesbury

DESTINATION DIEPPE

CHAPTER ONE

THE air in the room was hot and heavy. Hot with ill-controlled malign excitement; heavy with the acrid scents of human sweat, of stale tobacco smoke and of fear.

The Englishman, code name Gerard, his clothes in rags, his face bruised and pulpy, dark blood drooling out of one corner of his torn mouth, lay on the scuffed and stained bare boards of the floor panting, moaning softly, and struggling to rise. His dark eyes were glazed over with pain. He was barely conscious of what he was trying to do.

Above him ringing him round, were other men, his inquisitors; men with tight mouths and eyes which were too bright when they lingered on him. Men who had questioned him ceaselessly for eighteen hours; men without pity.

"Get him up!"

One man, small and thick-set, gave the order in German. Two others moved to obey.

Hard-fingered hands clamped on the prisoner's arms. He was lifted up and thrown back on to a wooden chair. His face was slapped, not gently, once, twice, three times. Breath hissed through his swollen lips. His head snapped around under the impact of each blow. Unwillingly his eyes focused.

"That's better," the small man said approvingly.

From overhead a brilliant light beat down upon the battlefield of the young man's face.

"Now –" the small, thick-set inquisitor went on, speaking in careful English " – now we begin all over again, eh?"

He paced across the floor unhurriedly to come to a halt, head up, legs astride, hands on hips, in front of his prisoner.

"We begin all over again, only this time – this time, Mr.

7

Gerard – " he lingered sibilantly over the name " – this time you are going to tell us what we want to know."

Gerard's torn mouth moved. Slowly he got out the words. "Go . . . to . . . hell . . ."

The small inquisitor's eyes flicked sideways. In answer, the hands of one of his companions drove downwards purposefully. Gerard screamed. It was a thin, inhuman sound.

The small man smiled. He said : "Why don't you grow up, Mr. Gerard? We are not children. We are not playing one of your stupid English games. We know that eventually you are going to answer our questions. By this time you must know it too. Why not answer them now? Why not be reasonable, eh?"

Gerard tried to shake his head. Hands seized him again. His body arched. Animal-like sounds rushed out from between his lips.

"Save yourself," the chief interrogator said softly. "Save yourself. Why do you endure this? For what? You must know that all your companions – all the *maquisards* we took with you – have talked. You think that they are as stupidly quixotic as you? They're not!"

Gerard's head dropped. One of the men standing by gripped it and forced it back. The Englishman's mouth gaped in anguish beneath the harsh glare of the overhead light.

"They've all talked – " the small inquisitor said in that same, soft, deadly voice " – all talked, every one of them. We know that the Anglo-Americans are going to invade. Even before your little group fell into our hands we knew that. But now we know where the invasion will take place – around Dieppe. That is what your brave companions told us. Now you are going to tell us when."

"No!" Gerard managed to get out. "No –"

"You're a fool, Mr. Gerard," the inquisitor said. "A stubborn fool. I'm giving you an opportunity to save yourself unnecessary suffering – pointless pain – and you are too

8

stupid to take it. You must know that we will have all our questions answered eventually. Either you will answer them – we will drag the answers out of you or kill you trying! – or someone else will – "

"Fug you!" Gerard said. "No – !"

The last word ended in a shriek as the small, thick-set inquisitor made an abrupt, impatient movement towards one of his companions and the man obeyed his unspoken command.

"No!" Gerard screamed. "No – ! No – !"

The interrogator turned his back on him.

The prisoner's screams ended as suddenly as they had begun.

"He's fainted, Herr Hauptmann."

"Revive him . . . and let him go."

The other's voice was incredulous. "Let him go, Herr Hauptmann?"

"Yes, but have him watched, constantly. I want to see what contacts he makes, if any."

Later that day Gerard walked, stiff-legged, out of the Gestapo Headquarters in Rouen, a temporarily free man.

*

The *Cafe des Deux Magots* was in Rouen – in German-occupied France. A calendar, crooked on a wall, gave the date as the twentieth of June, nineteen forty-two. The war was almost three years old, and going badly for the Allies; going well for the Germans. This last fact was underlined by the carefree ebullience of the German soldiers who crowded the cafe on this golden June afternoon.

Germany stood astride Europe, and Rommel was uncrowned king of North Africa. Only the previous day the Allied defenders of far-famed Tobruk had been finally overwhelmed by the Afrika Corps, and the Eighth Army under General Ritchie was falling back fast, and in some disorder back over the Egyptian border to Mersa Matruh.

In Russia, German forces had already swept like a tide over half a million square miles of Soviet territory, and were poised to blast their way further eastward again in a summer offensive. Behind the front in the Kursk-Kharkov sector, a gigantic army of two million men, fifty armoured divisions, and a vast fleet of bombers, dive-bombers and fighters had been assembled to carry the Germans relentlessly over the Don. In the south, in the Crimea, Kerch had been taken in the middle of May with a series of tremendous hammer blows delivered by six German infantry divisions and five hundred bombers. Other German forces were now pounding the fortress city of Sevastopol into ragged ruins and dust. The fortress had been under continuous attack for fifteen days now, and its fall was imminent. Its garrison had, by this time, been almost totally exterminated.

Everywhere, the fortunes of the Axis powers were in the ascendant. In the Far East, the armies of Imperial Japan had overrun Burma and were hammering on the very gates of India. In the *Cafe des Deux Magots* in occupied Rouen, in France, that June afternoon, German spirits were high; German laughter was loud.

But, beyond the Germans, at a tiny table deep in a shadowed and almost unnoticed corner, there was an island of ominous quiet. Here two civilians, a man and a woman, faced each other across the grubby, stained chequered cloth, and kept their voices down. When they spoke it was tensely, tautly, but very quietly. Out of thin, bitter mouths they dropped brief but barbed words into the deep pool of mutual distrust and animosity and suspicion which lay invisibly between them.

These two, this man and this woman, disliked each other intensely.

They disliked each other – the raven-haired and attractive young woman called Marianne, and the man with the pain-ravaged face – the man called Gerard – and they distrusted

10

each other. Yet they had to work together, side-by-side. More.

Each held the other's life in the hollow of their hand.

In any other job, or profession, the mutual distrust and animosity which existed between this young man and this woman might not have mattered; but it mattered here, and it mattered now. Mutual animosity, distrust and suspicion boded ill for one or the other of them – perhaps both.

They had not asked to work together. They had been ordered to work together. They did not like working together; they quarrelled bitterly. These were the cards dealt by fate.

In the *Cafe des Deux Magots*, in occupied Rouen, on this June afternoon, Marianne and Gerard argued in low voices, tensely, animosity flaring fiercely between them. It was animosity they could ill afford.

*

An old, senile waiter folded a bill and approached their table. Both Gerard and Marianne fell tautly silent.

Empty-eyed and morose, the waiter slid the bill beneath one of the near-cold, half-empty cups of ersatz coffee before them. Gerard's fingers reached for the bill, touched it, toyed with it. But he didn't look at Marianne again, nor did he speak until the old waiter had moved on.

Then he lifted his head and suddenly his weak mouth was set stubbornly. And he said: "I give the orders! You'll do what you're told to do! Is that clear?"

He said it harshly. His tone made her bridle afresh.

She said thinly: "But what you've told me to do is quite crazy. It's ridiculous! Besides, the Boche are watching you. Why else do you think they let you go? You're a danger to all of us."

"Nevertheless, you'll do as I say or – "

"Don't threaten me!" she said tautly. "You're in no

position to threaten anyone. You've got the kiss of death on you."

"You'll do it, or I'll report you to headquarters."

"I won't do it," she said flatly. "I'm not risking my life on a crackpot scheme like that one – I'm telling you! If you want it done, you'll just have to do it yourself. I think the treatment the Boche gave you has turned your head. You're not making sense any more."

Cold and quivering with anger, Gerard stood up. "If that's your attitude," he said harshly, "the sooner I get on to Headquarters the better."

Headquarters was in London, but it could be reached at any hour in an emergency by short-wave radio.

Marianne's eyes narrowed sharply. "Don't you dare! I'm warning you – you'll regret it!"

Gerard paused.

Marianne made him pause. His eyes, like hers, slid over the other people in the cafe. And his eyes were uneasy. Like her, whichever way he turned his head, he saw jackbooted German soldiers.

Then his mouth set and he sneered. "You don't frighten me!" For she couldn't mean it. Surely she wouldn't – she couldn't – betray him to the enemy, the Germans.

He stood there, leaning forward, still sneering, aggressive. "I'll give you one last chance. Are you going to do what – "

"You fool!" she flung at him. "You're under Gestapo surveillance. You may be picked up again any minute. Do you want to be caught in the act, at the transmitter – "

"I said we'll see what headquarters has to say," he flung back at her.

Both of them knew what headquarters in London would say. Gerard was in command. Right or wrong, his orders should be obeyed without question. This was the inflexible law which governed them. They were subject to a discipline as rigid as that of any military code.

12

If Gerard reported Marianne to headquarters in London, she would be recalled immediately – and in disgrace.

"You're being watched. I'm warning you – " she said again. But Gerard wasn't listening any longer. Blazingly, bitterly angry, he swung away from her. He paid the bill at the *patron's* desk near the door and then, without looking back, stalked furiously out into the street.

He walked two blocks before they caught up with him.

He thought then that Marianne must have carried out her threat and when the Germans called on him to halt he began to run. He was surprised that Marianne had betrayed him, and equally surprised that everything had happened so quickly; that the Germans had come after him so soon.

Running, detached from reality, he heard them shout after him. "*Halte, oder wir schiesen!* Halt! Halt, or we fire!"

He ran on.

He heard the sharp rattle of rifle bolts. He ducked his head and weaved from side to side. There was a bend in the road not more than twenty yards' distant. If he could reach it . . .

He saw a woman on the pavement in front of him suddenly twist away, horrified at what she could see happening behind him. He saw her throw herself flat across the child who was with her . . .

That was almost all that he knew.

The next instant he felt a tremendous blow across the back of his skull. He was aware of the ground spinning crazily in front of his falling eyes. He staggered.

"You bitch – !" he said thickly, without hearing the words and without even knowing he uttered them.

Then he fell.

There was blood on the road. Some of the windows along the street were starred and shattered. The child, beneath its mother on the pavement, was crying shrilly. The echoes of rifle-fire died.

The Gestapo men, walking stiffly, reached the young man called Gerard. One of them swung him over on to his back

13

He just lay there, sightless eyes open and staring.

The British agent called Gerard was dead.

*

Thirty kilometres north-west of Rouen, there was a large sprawling chateau which had been commandeered by the German Army. It was now a strongly guarded headquarters.

Polished boots heeled polished wood down an echoing hall.

An officer went quickly down the hall. A young officer, tall, fair-haired, faultlessly dressed in immaculate field-grey. He wore the insignia of a colonel of the German General Staff. The Knight's Cross of the Iron Cross showed at his breast.

He came to a door at the far end of the hall. A door guarded by a sentry who snapped to attention as the staff officer reached him. The sentry stood stiffly, not a muscle stirring, like a figure carved in stone, as the staff colonel tapped upon the door and received permission to enter.

In the room beyond, a lean whipcord figure in Field-Marshal's uniform moved between long windows splendid with sunshine and a large but severely planned desk.

The Field-Marshal was von Rundstedt, the master of the German defence system in the West. He was not a young man, but he gave every appearance of being a strong one. He was a professional soldier from the crown of his close-cropped iron-grey head to the soles of his mirror-polished boots.

"You have the information I wanted, Herr Oberst?"

The young staff colonel had it. In a file, he produced it. One of von Rundstedt's long, thin fingers traced a way through the typescript. "The Englishman, Gerard –"

"Dead, sir. He made a run for it. We couldn't risk his getting away."

14

"Damn trigger-happy, the Gestapo. And the others – ? Ah, I see we weren't quite as unlucky with all the others . . ."

"Two were taken alive, sir. The woman, of course, got away. The round-up has proceeded very satisfactorily."

"They have no idea who betrayed them?"

"None, sir."

"Good." The Field-Marshal straightened up. There was a brief silence. Then, pacing the floor, he said: "But nothing positive has resulted from the interrogations yet? The two taken alive have been interrogated?"

"The interrogations are still proceeding, sir. And both prisoners are proving obstinate. We have had to – "

The Field-Marshal stopped the young colonel abruptly. "I don't want to hear about it."

Again a brief silence.

" – But I do want results!"

Von Rundstedt had stopped in front of a large map of the French north-western coastline. It occupied almost the whole of one wall. It dominated the room.

Von Rundstedt said slowly and softly: "Something's in the wind – I know it. I can feel it in my bones. Those damned *Englanders* are up to something! But what? *What?* We've got to find out! We must!"

A hand jabbed forward. A fingernail scored a line beneath the name of a town.

"*Dieppe!* That's where they were planning to make a landing. But by now they may know that the plan isn't a secret any more. So where will the projected landing take place now? Or will it, in fact, take place at all? What will they do? Where will they strike?"

Von Rundstedt swung away from the map. He wheeled on the young colonel.

"We've got to be prepared for them if they do come. We've got to teach them a lesson they'll never forget. We can do it! All we need is a little foreknowledge. Every man throughout the whole of my command must be on his toes!"

CHAPTER TWO

RICHARD QUINTAIN was lean, rangy and muscular; a tall, dark, rakish man with a quick smile and a cleft to his chin.

He was tough, and he was relatively fearless most of the time – but not now. He was far from being fearless, at this particular moment in wartime London, in late June, nineteen forty-two.

His mouth and his throat were dry. He felt a sudden tightness within his chest, like iron-tipped, cold fingers closing over his heart. In all his thirty-eight years of life, though he'd known more than his share of hair-raising hazards and desperate situations, he'd never felt as nervous as he did at this moment.

Which, he told himself freely, was just plain ridiculous.

He stood on the threshold of the State Ballroom in Buckingham Palace, outwardly calm but inwardly very apprehensive indeed. He stood erect in the uniform of a Lieutenant-Colonel and, in front of him, the thin line of other uniformed men and women who were to be decorated before him was dwindling away.

His turn would come soon. Soon . . . soon . . . the word beat through his consciousness in time with the thudding of his heart.

There was a young woman immediately in front of him in the line; a slim, petite young woman wearing the uniform of an officer in the Nursing Yeomanry. A young woman with lustrous raven-black hair showing and glowing beneath her ugly uniform cap.

The lustrous raven-black hair was beautiful. The cap was not. The young woman herself could not, strictly, be called beautiful either, Quintain decided. But, without any doubt at all, she was very, very attractive.

16

She had dark eyes – intelligent eyes – quick to focus. In their depths there were shadows; strange shadows, Quintain saw, as she felt his gaze upon her and turned her head to look at him fleetingly and, just as fleetingly, smile.

He smiled back.

Then they were moving again. Moving more quickly now that they were inside the ballroom. Concealed somewhere close at hand, an orchestra played. A dozen impressions crowded in upon Quintain all at once. Impressions of the immensity of the ballroom and of a mass of faces turned towards his own. Impressions of a painted ceiling, of gilt and rich brocade and deep crimson carpeting. Impressions of bright, late June sunlight streaming in through high windows, and of a soft fragrance, bitter-sweet upon the senses, the subtle perfume of the young woman with the strangely shadowed eyes who had turned and looked at him – and smiled.

All the time they were moving. They reached a dais.

Now there was only the young woman in front of Quintain. The rest of the line had melted away. The young woman remained – the young woman and a group of high-ranking officers and Court officials on the dais itself.

In the midst of his officers stood the King, a slight, slim, almost boyish figure, only the fine lines around his mouth and eyes and the thin black mourning band which encircled his arm showing that he, too, had suffered loss.

His brother, George, Duke of Kent, had only recently been killed in an air crash. Death, no respecter of persons or position in this third year of war, had struck at almost every family in the kingdom.

The young woman in front of Quintain mounted the two richly carpeted steps to the dais, was received by the King, was decorated, and passed on.

Almost in a dream, Quintain found himself climbing the steps as she had done. An officer was holding a scroll, reading from it. A second high-ranking officer was holding a purple cushion on which a small, velvet-lined box was laid.

"*To Lieutenant-Colonel Quintain, for extraordinary services in war, above and beyond the call of duty . . .*"

The box was opened. The King took up the white enamelled gold cross that it contained and pinned it on Quintain's breast.

"Congratulations, Colonel."

"Thank you, Your Majesty."

A handshake. A stiff, formal bow both before and after his hand touched the hand of the King, and it was all over.

Quintain turned and went down the two steps from the dais. As he moved, the sunlight shafting in through the high windows glowed on the white, gold and crimson cross of the Distinguished Service Order on his breast.

"*For extraordinary services in war, above and beyond the call of duty . . .*"

Quintain found himself smiling a little wryly at that.

*

The ceremony over, Quintain went out into the courtyard of the palace.

And there he paused, on the very edge of the courtyard, his eyes crinkled against the bright sunlight. And still he was smiling a rather wry smile.

He had to, because he could still remember the words of the citation, and because he felt that, basically, they were untrue. This was why he had tried to refuse the decoration. Tried . . . and failed.

What he had done had not been "above and beyond the call of duty". He had been simply carrying out orders. And was what he had done so very extraordinary?

He had risked his life, and a newly-healed scar on his body – caused by a German bullet, which had laid bare a rib over his heart – showed what a real gamble that risk had been.

But other men were risking their lives in their country's service every second of every minute of every day, he thought, and not all of them collected decorations – not even posthumously. So what made him different?

He had gone into enemy-held territory, worked undercover in the country round St. Nazaire in France, and helped prepare the ground for the sensational and entirely successful Commando raid on the port on the night of the twenty-eighth of March, when the only graving dock on the French Atlantic seaboard capable of accommodating the capital ships of the German navy had been blown sky-high.

Yes, he conceded, perhaps there had been something just a little extraordinary in that.

For he had been landed, alone, on the St. Nazaire coast weeks ahead of the Commandos, and he had come out alone ten days after they had accomplished all the work that they'd set out to do. And, in the interval, alone, always alone – for he'd possibly been even more uncertain of the French in the area than he had been of the Germans – he'd kept London continually supplied with up-to-the-minute vital intelligence by short-wave transmitter, feeding the Combined Operations' Chiefs of Staff with the accurate information upon which the success of the entire operation would, must, and in fact did, wholly depend.

Even to himself, his sternest critic and taskmaster, Quintain could admit it hadn't been easy.

He had gone in constant danger of being located by the Germans in the middle of a transmission, for they could pick up his scrambled messages too, and they possessed excellent radio direction-finding apparatus with which to take a fix on his position. They had, in fact, nearly caught up with him on several occasions and, on the last, when he'd been interrupted in the middle of sending London a terse word-picture of the docks at St. Nazaire some days after the raid, he'd had his chest ploughed up by a bullet, and only narrowly escaped with his life.

Nevertheless, somehow staunching the flow of blood from the wound, somehow enduring the searing pain and somehow getting away from under the very nose of the German patrol with all his equipment intact, he had gone on to find a new hideout for himself and grimly completed his last, vital transmission.

But were these really "extraordinary services in war, above and beyond the call of duty" . . .?

And what of Felix Fenner – the man who had issued the orders which, at St. Nazaire, he had simply obeyed? Would Fenner consider what he had done in German-occupied France so very extraordinary?

Mentally Quintain shook his head and shook it emphatically.

Nothing was extraordinary to Fenner; nothing that he expected the men and the women who worked for him to do, nor in fact what they did.

The impossible had to be accomplished every day if you worked for a certain branch of British Intelligence and took your orders from Felix Fenner. Because nothing was extraordinary to Fenner. He lived in a world of readjusted values. For him the ordinary was something which simply did not exist.

"*It is because of Fenner and men like him* –" Quintain thought, with sudden insight, "*that we will win this war.*"

But he thought this unselfconsciously, because it did not occur to him that he and Felix Fenner were now almost two of a kind.

If this had been pointed out to him, Quintain would have laughed disparagingly. "*You don't understand . . .*" But the truth was that he had no notion of what effect war, and contact with Fenner, had had upon himself.

Since September, nineteen thirty-nine, his own values too, had been readjusted. In the twenty-three months which had followed, his character had undergone a subtle change.

In nineteen thirty-nine he had been largely unconscious of

20

his own shortcomings and imperfections – now he was very conscious of them, and of his limitations, too. But also, in nineteen thirty-nine, the word "can't" had had its place in his vocabulary. Now it had a place there no longer.

Like Fenner, in this late June of nineteen forty-two, he merely subconsciously divided the assignments he was given – no matter how hazardous – into those which could be done immediately, and those which might take a little longer.

Setting his shoulders, and tweaking his cap to a slight angle, he went across the courtyard of the Palace to the tall gates.

As he went, he had to skirt the crowd of relatives and friends of those who had just been decorated. They thronged the courtyard before the gates, congratulating their loved ones. For a moment – but only for a moment – Quintain felt something akin to loneliness tug at his heart.

From early childhood, in a country manse, brought up single-handed by a stern, strict disciplinarian of a father after his mother had deserted them both, he'd never had many close friends.

Passing out through the tall iron gates, the young woman who had been in front of him in the line at the Palace ceremony was in front of him still. She had smiled at him once, and now she did so again. A very attractive young woman . . . raven-haired, petite and with excellent legs . . . slim . . .

Quintain hesitated. It seemed that the woman had nobody waiting here for her either. And she would have time on her hands. She was bound to have time on her hands. One was always given a few extra days leave for an investiture.

It was a pity that, though he must have heard her name read out immediately before she'd been decorated, he couldn't remember it. Still . . .

He moved towards her. She hesitated too, in her turn. She was obviously waiting for him.

And then something happened.

An Army officer climbed out of a closed black car parked

21

on the other side of Constitution Hill. Climbed out and waved and called out: "*Hello there –*"

The young woman turned her head away from Quintain. She saw the Army officer as he waved again. She began to walk towards him.

"Damn!" thought Quintain almost fiercely. The moment was lost.

Mentally shrugging, he turned away. Well, maybe it hadn't been such a good idea after all. Maybe this was fate intervening . . .

And then he stopped.

There was the sound of running feet behind him. "*Wait a moment, sir! Wait –*"

Puzzled, Quintain swung around. The Army officer was chasing *him* now!

"*Just a moment, sir!*"

The woman was standing beside the long black car talking to someone inside it through a half-open door. Talking to someone Quintain could not see.

He frowned.

As he waited for the Army officer, a Provost major, to come up to him, he wondered what was happening. Not an identity card check, surely! Everything would be explained if this were an identity card check. But what fool of the Provost Marshal's Branch would seek to find spies and saboteurs leaving Buckingham Palace after an investiture?

The major reached Quintain, panting. He was fat and sandy-haired, middle-aged and out of condition. "Lieutenant-Colonel Quintain?"

"Yes –?"

Quintain was surprised that the Provost Major should know his name.

"Would you come with me, sir?" The major gestured. "Would you come over to the car?"

"Why?" Quintain asked. It seemed like a good question.

22

"Please come with me, sir," the major insisted. Quintain hesitated, then shrugged. Not speaking, he crossed the road at the major's side.

High overhead, like silver fish swimming in a cobalt sea, heavy bombers droned a path to France.

Quintain and the major reached the car. The woman was still standing there. She was leaning forward talking to someone through the half-open door. Quintain and the major came up behind her.

Who was she talking to? What was all this about?

Then Quintain knew.

For the young woman moved back half a pace, and now Quintain could see into the car. And now, too, he knew what kind of a man it was who would seek spies and saboteurs leaving Buckingham Palace.

The answer was – Felix Fenner's kind of man. The man in the car *was* Fenner.

His spare frame occupied a small part of the back seat. He leaned back against the leather cushions in the rear of the car and regarded Quintain with some amusement. His old eyes were bright in his thin, heavily lined, ascetic face. "Wondered what was happening, did you?"

He produced the inevitable Egyptian cigarette, fitted it into a long holder, lit it, and gestured with it. He was gesturing towards the woman in Nursing Yeomanry uniform. "You've met Marianne." It was more of a statement than a question. His bright blue eyes glittered. His voice had its usual rasp.

Then, abruptly, the smile left his thin, ascetic face. "I'm glad that you've met her," he said. "You'll be working with her. Now get in."

"Working . . . ?" Quintain echoed.

Fenner snorted. "You don't think that just because you're some kind of perishing hero you're not going to do any more work?"

23

"No, of course not –"

"Then get in!" Fenner said shortly. "Get in – come on –
both of you!"

"Both of you have recently come out of Occupied France,"
he went on, when they were seated in the car, "and both of
you are going back there soon. Very soon. So we have a lot
to talk about, and more to do."

He snapped his thin fingers and glared at the Provost
Marshal. "Come on, man! Come on! We haven't all day!"
And the Provost Major hastily scuttled round the car and
clambered in behind the wheel. "Take your finger out, man!"
Fenner roared, his ginger beard bristling. "Get this heap
moving!"

CHAPTER THREE

His denim overalls bunched and baggy, Quintain hunched himself forward, webbing cutting into him, the parachute heavy as lead on his back.

He sat with his booted feet braced against the metal ridge which ran around the opening in the belly of the aircraft. A cold, wet wind sliced up through the opening, stiffening the skin of his face.

Around him the air was filled with shuddering noise as the engines of the Halifax bomber began to slow their beat. Opposite him, sitting on the other side of the hole in the floor, trussed up in denims and parachute pack and webbing as he was, her face a little pale now – paler than he had ever known it, now that the moment awaited for three long weeks was actually here – Marianne tried to summon up a smile for him.

Quintain smiled back.

Below them, not far below them, seen quite clearly through the opening in the floor as a moonlit land across which the shadow of their Halifax skimmed and scudded, was France – Occupied France.

And, soon, they would be going down there, Quintain thought. Soon the stolid, seemingly unimaginative Royal Air Force flight-sergeant who now stood above them phlegmatically and interminably chewing gum, would check the clips on the end of their static lines for one last time, would bellow to each to be ready, and would anxiously watch the two small lamps screwed to a bracket above the opening in the floor.

Both lamps were dark at this moment, but soon, any second now, one of them would burn red. This would mean that the aircraft's bomb-aimer had sighted the place where his human cargo and the accompanying equipment had to be dropped.

The red light was a warning light. The rest would follow inevitably.

The pilot would circle the dropping ground once. On the first time round the containers of equipment would be dropped. Then the aircraft would level off for a second run-in.

That was when the despatcher would become tense, and the seconds would thump by agonizingly. Then the green light would flash, and the despatcher would scream a command as his hand fell, and Marianne would tumble out into space first, and he would follow.

That was what would happen. That was what had been planned to happen. This they had planned and rehearsed and gone over again and again for three weeks. Ever since that morning he had been summoned to meet Felix Fenner in the big black car outside Buckingham Palace.

Poised on the edge of action now, his muscles and nerves taut and hard, Quintain dragged his mind away from the pressing present and the urgent future, and thought about England and about Fenner.

Flying over France, only minutes – perhaps only seconds – away from the leap he knew he must take, following the canisters down into the moonlit unknown, he thought about the things that had happened; the things which Fenner had said to him only a few weeks before in London, the things which had brought him, inexorably, to this place, this plane, and this moment in time.

"It's a very tough assignment I have to offer you," Fenner had rasped. "A very tough and very dirty job indeed!"

Quintain and Marianne had been in the back of the big black car, on either side of Fenner's frail figure. The maples and sycamores of Constitution Hill had been sliding past the darkened windows.

"Marianne will know just how tough and how danger-

26

ous –" Fenner had continued, moving searching blue eyes in her direction "– when I tell you that I propose to have you both dropped into France near Gournay en Bray."

"But that's where –" Marianne had begun, with an abrupt movement. And then, just as suddenly, she had stopped.

"Exactly, my dear." Fenner had stroked his red beard very gently, and his voice had been soft and silky; even dangerously soft and silky, Quintain thought. "Exactly, that is precisely where you have just returned from. I know."

He had twisted around to explain to Quintain: "Marianne was with the Maquis until only just recently. She was operating in the Gournay en Bray region – not far from Rouen. Then things became a little . . . a little too hot, eh, Marianne?"

Fenner had chuckled, but it had been a humourless sound.

"In two short days everything went to pieces. Another of my agents, a young man called Gerard, who was operating with the same Maquis group, was killed by the Germans under rather . . . well, rather peculiar circumstances. Almost immediately afterwards the Maquis was ambushed, and not many of its members escaped. Fortunately, Marianne was one of the few who did. I ordered her back here to give me a full report – naturally. In the meantime, other things have been happening. Things which make it imperative –" and again Fenner's brilliant blue eyes slid away from Quintain to consider the young woman thoughtfully "– things which make it imperative for me to ask her to return to Gournay en Bray once more – with you."

Marianne had said nothing. She had seemed, Quintain thought, to be tensed, as if waiting for something further to be said, or something to happen before speaking.

But nothing did happen. And, for a long moment, nothing further was said.

Then, slowly, very very slowly indeed, Fenner shifted his gaze back to Quintain.

He said quietly: "There are one or two things I must make

27

plain. The first is that the successful completion of the assignment I have to offer you is of vital importance. And the second is that it would be a difficult assignment to carry out at any time, but with the Germans in the Gournay en Bray area wary and watchful, as Marianne can tell you they are, the task I want you to undertake becomes more than difficult. It becomes almost impossible."

He stopped then, and a long moment dragged by. Then he looked at both of them quickly, in turn. "Before I tell you anything else, you are entitled to refuse this assignment – either one or both of you. Do you refuse it?"

"No."

Quintain and Marianne said the word together, almost in unison. Almost – but not quite. Marianne said it quickly. More quickly than Quintain. A little too quickly – as if she wanted to get it out without thinking about it. Both men looked at her, Fenner inscrutably, Quintain curiously. Her eyes were empty. Her expression was guarded. It told them nothing.

There was a millesecond's silence, and then Felix Fenner said: "Very well . . ."

In front of them, in the driver's seat of the big black car, the Provost Major kept his hands lightly on the wheel, and his eyes on the unreeling road ahead.

"What I have to tell you, and what you must do," Fenner said simply, "is concerned with a full-scale dress-rehearsal invasion of Europe which is planned to take place very shortly."

*

Silence.

Somewhat stunned silence.

Then Quintain said: "Concerned with – a *what?*"

"With a full-scale landing on the coast of France," Fenner told him. "Something much, much bigger than that last affair you were involved in at St. Nazaire. This operation is to begin with the seizure of a strongly defended enemy port by frontal assault, and is to involve penetration of the enemy coastline in depth. Over ten thousand men are going to be employed in this. Ten thousand men, backed up by destroyers, aircrafts and tanks. It's going to be the biggest Combined Operation to date."

"But, for all that, a rehearsal –?" Quintain's tone was frankly incredulous. "A rehearsal, you said –?"

"A rehearsal for the invasion of Europe. Yes."

"Which means that our men are landed, do what they have to do, and are then taken off again – like at St. Nazaire?"

"That's right."

"Ten *thousand* men?"

"About six thousand will actually land."

"And what have they got to do?"

"Take an airfield, destroy some batteries, cut out some German invasion barges to be towed back, and hold an enemy port for six hours."

Fenner's thin-featured, bearded face was expressionless.

Quintain said bluntly: "For Pete's sake – why?"

"I told you."

"A dress rehearsal, you said. And when are we actually invading Europe? The week after the dress-rehearsal?"

"Of course not!"

"The week after that, then? The next month?"

"Maybe next year," Fenner said roughly. "But more likely –"

"– the year after that," Quintain said. "I know. You've no need to tell me. Anyone who knows anything understands that we have neither the men nor the war materials to invade for months yet – perhaps years yet! Then, I repeat, why this so-called 'dress-rehearsal'? What's the point?"

"Are you arguing that we won't gain anything from an assault in strength?" Fenner inquired rather tartly.

"We might learn a lot," Quintain said. "But is what we learn going to be any use to us? By the time we apply what we've learned, conditions will have changed. This dress-rehearsal invasion of ours will have helped the Germans learn, too."

"Then you don't think much of the plan?" Fenner inquired.

"I don't think anything of it," Quintain said bluntly. "Some of the top brass obviously have chessboard fever. Ten thousand pawns to be put on a certain square and then taken off again –"

"Six thousand," Fenner said gently. He stroked his red beard.

"Six thousand – five thousand – what's the difference? You've told me the jobs they have to do. Two companies of Commandos –"

"Could do them? Yes . . ." Fenner said, and the words lingered. Then he went on: "But the objectives themselves aren't all that important. It's the exercise –"

He stopped abruptly.

He shook his head wonderingly. He growled: "I'm damned if I know what I'm defending the plan for. I don't have to . . ."

He said: "I agree with you that whichever way you look at it, logically, it's crazy. It will prove nothing and demonstrate nothing which could not be proved or demonstrated in some other less dangerous and less expensive way."*

*On April 4th 1942, General Marshall and Harry Hopkins flew to London to confer with Churchill. They came as Roosevelt's emissaries.

Everywhere, the war was going badly for the Allies. Particularly in Russia. And Stalin had let it be known that, if needs be, he wouldn't hesitate to seek a separate peace with Germany. To this end, he had already tried to convey to the Germans that, despite everything, he was far from being an implacable enemy.

"The Red Army," he had declared on 23rd February 1942, "has no desire to exterminate the German nation, nor destroy the German state."

Roosevelt was worried.

For some months, he had had a newly promoted and completely unknown general drawing up American plans for the war. This general's name was Dwight D. Eisenhower, and the plans which he produced at the end of March 1942 envisaged the invasion of Europe in that same year, with Britain bearing the full brunt of the attempt.

And he sighed.

"I agree it's never necessary to stick one's head into a lion's mouth just to satisfy oneself that all big cats have teeth. But –"

And he stopped again. After that his voice hardened.

"Whatever we think of the plan does not matter," he said. "What does matter is that the plan is on. The decisions have been made. The exercise, the assault, the raid – call it what you will – will certainly take place!"

He looked up. He eyed Quintain steadily.

"And your job, and Marianne's, and mine," he said, "is to see that casualties are kept down to a minimum. That, basically, is the objective of everything I am going to ask you to do in France. We must work to keep casualties *down*!"

His voice was grim.

"And we may have a very hard job," he said then. "I think, in fact, that it will be a particularly hard job for us all. For –" and his bright blue eyes were cold, and they were bleak "– all the information I have tells me that the Germans know our boys are coming!"

Roosevelt had given these proposals his approval on April Fool's Day 1942. Now, on April 4th, Marshall and Hopkins flew to London to force them on Churchill.

Remarkably well-informed of what was in the wind, the Germans laughed at the idea. Chortled Radio Paris: "Roosevelt has given Hopkins and Marshall full powers to provide Great Britain with all the help she might need to try a second Narvik – short of actually sending American troops, of course. Churchill should be warned that, in attempting a second Narvik, he risks a second Dunkirk."

Churchill, in fact, was well aware of it.

There were 25 German divisions stationed in France and the Low Countries. Even if the aircraft and landing craft were available, Britain had only 10 trained divisions to operate on the Continent and, until the autumn, the Americans could only spare two.

Nevertheless, after 10 days' discussion, Churchill gave his consent to the plan: a limited invasion of Europe in 1942. And Hopkins and Marshall delightedly returned to Washington to inform Roosevelt of all the decisions reached.

Here was the answer to Stalin's demand for "a Second Front *now*" to take the weight off his hard-pressed armies.

Churchill, however, had no intention of executing the American

31

plan unless the situation on the Russian Front threatened an immediate collapse of the Red Army, and he intimated as much to Molotov, when the Soviet Foreign Minister arrived in London on May 20th to find out the date planned for the promised Second Front.

Considerably disgruntled, Molotov went on to Washington, where he did not hide his fears that the Red Army would be unable to withstand the German Summer Offensive unless a Second Front was mounted at once. In which case, he informed Roosevelt grimly, a negotiated peace between Russia and Germany would be inevitable.

Roosevelt reacted.

After taking General Marshall's advice, he authorized Molotov to tell Stalin it was intended to open a Second Front that year.

Whatever the cost, Roosevelt thereafter insisted to Churchill, a landing of some sort must be made on the shores of Europe in 1942. Even if it was what he called "a sacrifice landing".

And it so happened that, just at that moment, a raid on Dieppe was being considered by the Combined Operations Planning Staff.

Now preparations were pushed ahead.

The date of the raid was first fixed for 4th July 1942. Significant timing? But then, because of continuing bad weather, it had to be called off. But not before troops had embarked, and been told where they were going.

After this, it was confidently expected by all that the raid would be completely dropped. The troops had been told where they were going, and what was afoot, and now that they were dispersed the secret was heavily compromised. General Montgomery, in command of the operation at this time, thought it was reasonable to suppose that the raid-that-never-was had become a general topic of conversation in all the pubs on the south coast, for in addition to the 5,000 Canadian soldiers, a number of sailors and airmen had been involved. "As soon as the force had been dispersed," he remarks, "I considered that the operation had been cancelled and turned my attention to other questions."

But Combined Operations Headquarters was of a different opinion, and Mountbatten succeeded a few days later in having the principles of a new expedition to Dieppe approved by the Committee of Chiefs of Staff.

Can the reason for this have been that the thought had crossed someone's mind that, whatever happened, a raid on Dieppe might fill the bill very nicely? It would show the Russians and the Americans – both pressing for action – that, in deference to their demands, something had been attempted, but that it wasn't easy to set foot on enemy-held coast.

CHAPTER FOUR

"The Germans know –?" Quintain was aghast. "You mean, they know when and where . . . .?"

Fenner was nodding. "I mean," he said positively, interrupting, "that this operation has been in the wind far too long. Too many people have been taken into the confidence of the planning staff. There has been too much careless talk. This operation was planned as far back as April, and originally scheduled for one day next week. But for various reasons it was called off. However, it's now on again. On the night of August the eighteenth and the morning of the nineteenth as the time, and with the same target as before – Dieppe!"

"Dieppe!" Quintain exclaimed. "But isn't that –"

"A heavily defended port? More strongly defended than even St. Nazaire was? It always has been!"

"And the Germans *know?*"

"I believe so. Consider this, and tell me what you think." Fenner leaned forward, beard jutting aggressively.

"When the plan was first mooted, back in April," he said, "there were only fourteen hundred second-grade German troops in Dieppe. A week ago, in good time to meet our projected assault – had it gone ahead completely as planned – these troops were replaced by others – a crack division. In addition, the Tenth Panzer Division is standing by on the outskirts of the town, together with the SS Division *Adolf Hitler* – and these babies are as tough as they come."

Fenner's voice was low.

"And that is the situation at this moment. But consider this, too. When our assault was called off, some of the frontline troops in and around Dieppe were withdrawn. Then the plan, instead of being thrown overboard entirely, was merely

33

put back for some weeks. *That was when the German front-line troops returned to the town."*

"The Germans have a good Intelligence service," Quintain said sourly.

"Of course! And why not? They're not fools! Good God –!" Fenner's voice rasped out in bitterness. "You know what our security arrangements are like! Practically non-existent! So it is as I have said. Too many people in this country have long known of the plan to attack Dieppe. There has been too much loose talk. We put up funny little notices – *'Be Like Dad – Keep Mum'* – but no one regards them very seriously. Why they're even designed and executed by cartoonist from the comic papers. A laugh in every line! They're just so many official jokes pasted up on the walls of railway waiting rooms and public bars. They don't mean anything – and so men die . . ."

His voice tailed off.

He said heavily: "Anyway, for better or for worse, the assault on Dieppe is going to take place as planned. Exactly as planned. And that is where you and Marianne come into the picture."

Marianne? Quintain had almost forgotten about her. She had remained silent for so long. He looked at her, and then back at Fenner. He asked the question as much for her as for himself. "What do you want us to do?"

"I'm going to have you dropped into France near Gournay en Bray. I can get you no nearer to the coastal defences. At Gournay, you will contact the remnants of the Maquis that Marianne served with. You must weld those remnants into an instrument of war – an instrument which can be used . . ."

Fenner looked up.

"There is an E-boat base to the east of Dieppe. It is four kilometres beyond Puys, seven kilometres from Dieppe itself, and about sixty-one kilometres from Gournay. That E-boat base you must utterly destroy! I told you that your

34

mission was concerned with saving life and reducing casualties in our assault on Dieppe. It is. The E-boat base must be obliterated immediately before our men attack the town, so that the Germans will be unable to harry them from the sea–"

He leaned forward, his glance flickering between Marianne and Quintain. He spoke slowly and positively.

"When I tell you that over two hundred and fifty little ships will be taking part in our operation against Dieppe – two hundred and fifty little ships indifferently armed – you will be well able to imagine the chaos and havoc which could ensue if the E-boats were permitted to roam loose amongst them."

His voice was hard. His beard jutted.

"This must not happen! A destroyer screen, operating in mid-Channel, will prevent enemy reinforcements arriving on the scene. Your job it to take care of the only enemy naval forces on the spot. Is that understood? You must take care of them! There can be no slip-ups or errors. This is vitally important. The E-boats must be accounted for."

He leaned back. He said sombrely: "The lives of hundreds – perhaps thousands – of our boys will be in your hands. You must not fail. Whatever happens to the operation as a whole, *you* must not fail!"

Quintain exhaled breath lingeringly. "So that's the job! Attack the base or –"

"Dynamite it!"

"And to do it we have only the remnants of one demoralized Maquis to assist us."

Fenner didn't say anything. He merely nodded.

"A tall order," Quintain said. "A tough assignment –" and laughed, though he didn't feel like laughing. "You certainly do hand out some dirty ones!"

"I told you it would be dangerous and difficult," Fenner said. And then: "Nor does it end there. I have one other job for you. For you alone . . ."

He had paused then. The big black car had just slid

through the open gates in front of the Natural History Museum, South Kensington. It purred gently round the crescent-shaped drive, and braked to a halt at the foot of broad steps.

"For you alone," Fenner had repeated. "Come with me. Marianne will wait for you."

And he had prised himself out of the car and gone up the steps and into the museum with Quintain hard on his heels.

*

The museum had long since been closed to the public. An emergency measure. Precious exhibits had been packed off to places of safety throughout the country. The great, gaunt building remained to be used as a vast headquarters, nerve-centre and advanced training school for, amongst others, Felix Fenner's own private army of secret agents – nominally a branch of British Military Intelligence, but in actual fact accountable only and directly to one of Fenner's personal friends, His Majesty's Secretary of State for War.

And there, once in Fenner's private office, past all the check points and guards and the lusciously ripe redheaded secretary stationed, conveniently, in the ante-room, the door had been locked and then Quintain and Fenner talked.

How they had talked!

But Quintain, much as he wanted to remember, had to forget what they had talked about now. He had to forget the grim surprises that the small, bearded man had had in store for him.

He had to forget because the red light had been burning above the gaping rectangular hole in the floor of the Halifax bomber for all of twenty seconds, and the plane had done one run over the dropping zone. The canisters had gone out and down. Now there was no room in Quintain's mind for anything but what he must do in the immediate future.

"*Ready?*" the despatcher bawled in his ear.

Quintain nodded.

Opposite him, Marianne tensed herself.

"*Ready . . . ?*"

At the end of its run the plane had banked and come round. Through the hole in the floor Quintain could see four lights on the ground below. Four small lights. Hand torches, probably. They made the shape of a diamond. One of them was flashing an erratic "B" – the morse code letter for the drop.

Quintain dragged his eyes away.

He remembered what he had been told.

Don't look at the signal lamps above the opening. Don't look at the ground scudding beneath the opening in the aircraft's belly. Don't look at anything but the despatcher's hand. Watch it closely. It's raised now. When it falls . . .

"*Go!*" snarled the despatcher, stolid and phlegmatic no longer. "*Go!*"

Marianne went head first through the opening like a swimmer diving into a moonlit milky sea. Quintain followed her without allowing himself to think or to hope – or even to pray.

He followed her, and the slipstream knifed him, taking his breath away as he tumbled through space. Then, with a crack like a pistol-shot, the parachute opened above him.

He swung like a giddy pendulum. He looked around him, looking for Marianne through the moonlit night, and not seeing her. He felt naked in the silver air. Naked and defenceless. He'd never done a jump before. Always in the past he'd been landed in enemy territory from a submarine. He wasn't sure that he liked jumping.

He felt that every German in France must be looking upward, must see him dangling – a wonderful and helpless target for any crack shot with a rifle.

Then, with a jarring shock, he hit earth, and as he had been taught, he immediately rolled.

He was back in Occupied France.

CHAPTER FIVE

VOICES carved the night apart. Harsh voices shouting to each other. Urgent voices, some of them French, but at least one of them unmistakably thick and guttural – alien.

Quintain heard them and reacted to them before the roar of the returning aircraft swallowed them up.

He had landed on rough ground by the side of a canal. He had no idea where Marianne was, but he did know that there should be a reception committee of French Resistance fighters waiting for them. The remnants of a Maquis. The voices he heard could belong to them. They had pinpointed the dropping ground for the pilot of the Halifax, and now they were looking for Marianne and himself.

This was one theory.

Another which flashed through Quintain's mind was that no *maquisard* had pinpointed this drop at all. It had happened before. All it needed was for the Germans to get wind of the drop and break the code letter out of somebody, and they were in business – and he was in trouble.

This was a thought which Quintain found distinctly unpleasant.

It was the gutturally alien – almost Germanic voice he had heard which occasioned the thought, and which worried him. That, and the fact that the owners of the voices were moving around without caution – even shouting to one another.

In all Quintain's experience of Occupied France at night, only Germans ever shouted. If the men he could hear were really and truly the remnants of a Maquis badly mauled by the enemy would they run even the remotest risk of drawing attention to themselves in this way?

The more Quintain thought about what was happening,

the less he liked it. If the men he could hear were Germans, they were hunting him now. And hunting Marianne. Where *was* she?

The French voice he had heard could belong to men of the *Milice*, the German sponsored French police, just as easily as to men of the Resistance.

As the Halifax roared low over the dropping ground and then climbed into the moonlit night at the end of its run, Quintain didn't know what to think. He didn't know what the owners of the voices were – friends or foes.

He took no chances.

Swiftly he gathered up his parachute, bundling it. He stripped off his webbing harness and the denims beneath and thrust everything out of sight under some nearby bushes.

The Halifax was now silhouetted against the stars. It dipped its wings once in salute and farewell and then it was gone, the sound of its engines a fast-receding grumble in the milky moonlit sky.

Quintain lay close to the earth, and his Webley pistol, ready to fire, was hard in his hand. He lay close to the earth and he waited as the voices he had heard resumed their speech above and around him, hunting over the ground, coming closer to where he was.

If the men he could hear – the men now approaching – were Germans or in the employ of the Germans, they would not take him alive. The knuckle of his right index finger was white on the trigger of his gun as he waited tensely.

He was prepared to sell his life and his liberty very dearly if need be. But – and the question was more urgent than ever now – where was Marianne?

What was she doing? What had happened to her?

*

Quintain could think back now.

As his eyes probed the night, and as he waited for the

owners of the voices around him to come closer still, he could remember how Felix Fenner had surprised him, grimly, in the vast high-ceilinged room, baronial in its dimensions, which he had set apart as his office in the Natural History Museum.

Office . . .? It was the size of a rifle range!

The door had been locked. At the other end of the vast room there had been no-one to overhear them. Looking out and down from the window he had seen Marianne still sitting in the back of the big black car parked in front of the museum's entrance.

Then Fenner's voice had reached him, harshly and urgently: "*Take care* –!"

He had swung round at that.

More than one question had crowded into his eyes.

Fenner had been looking at him – strangely. " I told you I had an extra-special job for you, Quintain. A job for you alone –"

He had stood by Quintain's side at the window, looking down too. He had been small and brooding; malignant. "Watch *her!*" he had said.

Quintain had been more than a little surprised.

"Never turn your back on her if you can avoid it!" Fenner had bitten the words off, making them ugly. "Never let her out of your sight for a moment."

"Marianne –?" Quintain had got out. "But –"

"I know she's one of my operatives. And I know I ought to be able to trust her, and tell you to trust her." Fenner's face had been as hard as his voice. "But I can't."

"But –" Quintain's hands had opened and closed helplessly "– but she was at the investiture this morning!"

"I recommended her for that decoration myself," Fenner had said roughly. "Not my usual practice – as you know. But I wanted to reassure her."

"I don't think I understand."

Fenner had looked at Quintain then. He had eyed him

40

directly, and it had seemed as if his red beard had bristled. "Don't you? I thought I was making myself perfectly clear. Isn't it obvious? I suspect our Marianne of being a double-agent. Of working for the Germans as well as for me."

Quintain had stared.

Fenner said shortly: "Gerard Heller was betrayed, you know. Someone put the finger on him for the Germans. That someone could have been Marianne."

"But not only Marianne, surely –" Quintain was astounded by everything Fenner was saying. He had known this man a long time – but never known him as hard and as cold-eyed as this. He felt forced to rise to Marianne's defence. "If Gerard was betrayed, couldn't any member of the Maquis have done it?"

"Any member could," Fenner agreed. "The question is – why should they?"

"Why should Marianne?"

"They were mutually antagonistic," Fenner said. "They were continually at loggerheads. They disliked each other intensely."

"But surely –" Quintain began to protest.

"A woman wouldn't betray a man just for that reason?" Fenner finished for him. "I agree. Not for that reason alone. But my own sources of information tell me that Gerard was constantly provoking Marianne into acts of insubordination, and that he had threatened to report her for refusing to carry out orders. If he had reported her, of course –" Fenner shrugged "– I'd have been bound to recall her. Gerard Heller was in command. I'd have had to back him up . . ."

"She'd have been recalled in disgrace, you mean?" Quintain said.

"I mean," Fenner replied, "that if she knew he was about to report her for insubordination, it might well have been the last straw. There was so much bad blood between them already. She might have betrayed him. And he *was* betrayed. This I can state quite certainly."

Quintain was still surprised at the turn events had taken. "But if you suspect her of going over to the enemy, why are you sending her on this mission with me?"

Fenner moved slightly and growled: "Of course I'm not one-hundred-per-cent sure. If I was, I'd know what to do with Marianne, and I'd do it. That I promise you!" His blue eyes were very bleak. He said: "I know how to deal with proven traitors . . ."

There, briefly, he paused.

Then he said: "All I know with certainty is what I've told you – that Gerard Heller was betrayed to the Germans in Rouen. The rest seems to follow. I wish it didn't. All the other people working with the Gournay Maquis were comparatively old hands at the game, and before this there'd been no slip-ups, certainly no betrayals. Marianne was the only newcomer to the Maquis, its one untried member – and this happens. The Maquis is sold out to the Germans –"

Fenner sighed.

"As for why I'm sending her back to France with you – well, surely the answer to that's obvious enough. If Marianne did betray Gerard Heller, she must be working for the Germans now. I don't know whether she is or she isn't. I have no way of knowing – until I give her another job of work to do and send her back to France. If I kept her here, I couldn't use her. I'd never know whose side she was really on. By sending her back to France I'm giving her the chance to make contact with the Germans again. I'm giving her a chance to show her hand."

"And what am I supposed to do while she's proving herself?" Quintain asked roughly. "You said yourself that the job you've given me to do in France is a very important one. How can I do it properly –"

"– with a traitor working beside you?" Fenner finished for him. "Somehow, you're going to have to do it, for if Marianne isn't working for the Germans someone else at Gournay is!"

42

He lit a cigarette with an abrupt movement. He narrowed his intensely blue eyes against the smoke which climbed his thin, bearded face. He said brusquely: "Of course it's going to be difficult. Very difficult. Didn't I say so? Difficult – but necessary. I have to prove Marianne one way or the other. That's vital. If she betrayed Gerard she can betray other people – and other things. Codes, plans, rendezvous, other Maquis – maybe she has done so already. I want to know!"

He let ash fall from his cigarette. Broodingly he scuffed it into the carpet which surrounded his desk. "On the other hand," he said, "it's not going to be quite as difficult as I purposely made it appear."

"And what does that mean?"

"I told you the plan for Dieppe in front of Marianne because there was nothing to lose and everything to gain by letting her think I still trust her. The Germans already know all there is to know about it anyway. I'm sure of that. As for the rest – your own special assignment –"

"The E-boat base –?"

Fenner nodded. "The E-boat base. You are responsible for its destruction, as I said. But not *directly* responsible."

"You're going to have to explain."

"It did no harm to let Marianne think that you would be engineering the destruction of the base personally. If she's in cahoots with the enemy, she'll pass on the information and the Germans will be so busy looking outward, watching for you, that they will overlook the activities of the men who are really going to do the damage – French civilians working *inside*. Men whom Jerry thinks he can trust, and who he's employing around the base."

Fenner gestured with his long Egyptian cigarette.

"Your job is still an important one. It is to contact these French civilians and supply them with the explosives they'll need for their task. But –"

"But nothing!" Quintain said rudely. "Is that all?"

43

Fenner stared at him. "Is that all . . .?" he echoed. "Is that all . . . he says!"

And Fenner laughed.

"Yes, that's all. All you have to do is collect enough explosive to obliterate a fair-sized town. You'll need that much because the E-boats are safe and secure in their concrete pens and the only way to be sure of them is to blow up the lot. Just that – and deliver it to the men who are going to do the job –"

Quintain made to speak, and Fenner stopped him. "I haven't finished. I want to point out to you that both the collection of the explosive and its delivery are problems in themselves. This fact may have escaped you, but it's true. It's true because – first – the R.A.F. can't guarantee to deliver enough 'soup' for the job at any one time and place before August the eighteenth, when it will be needed, so you're going to have to scour Northern France for existing, stale supplies. And it's true because – second – in order to get it to the sabotage team, you're going to have to breach some of the strongest coastal defences in the world.

"And if these weren't problems enough," he continued, "you have the fact that if you're handling stale explosive it will undoubtedly be unreliable – threatening to go up at any moment – and also that you'll be working under the noses of the Germans all the time.

"Added to which, of course," he went on sarcastically, "if you still crave for excitement, you can comfort yourself with the thought that there is certainly going to be a traitor sitting at your elbow watching every move you make so that it can be reported back to the Germans. Does that satisfy you–?"

"I –"

Again Fenner cut Quintain short. "Does that satisfy you? It ought to! That's all you have to do, by God! But – isn't it enough?"

Quintain was grinning now. "Why did I open my big mouth!"

Slowly, Fenner smiled. He moved then, and Quintain moved with him. At the door, Fenner hesitated as he thrust out his thin, skeletal hand in a gesture of farewell.

"I'll see you again, of course, before you're dropped. Many times. You'll be thoroughly briefed. In the meantime –" and his voice came out strongly "– watch Marianne. Don't be caught napping, that's all. I hope I'm wrong about her. I'd like to be wrong about her. I'm rather fond of her –"

Seeing the expression of Quintain's face, Fenner had said again: "I *am* rather fond of her, but I can't let any affection I may feel for her blind me."

He had shrugged thin shoulders, tugged at his beard, brooded a moment. "Weak though he was, I was rather fond of Gerard, too . . ."

All this, Quintain remembered.

But at that point his memories faded, dying as Felix Fenner's voice had died. There was no time for thoughts of the past. The problems of the present were now too pressing.

He was lying close to the earth near a canal in Northern France, and his Webley was hard in his hand –

– And armed men, strangers, were almost upon him.

*

The men came across the uneven ground in a thin, straggling line, like beaters at a rough shoot, bent on flushing game.

They carried their weapons at high port, rifles or Stens, and there were thirteen men in the party. Unlucky thirteen, Quintain thought. His hand came up and his Webley was in it, and the safety-catch was definitely off.

Unlucky thirteen . . . for they were making far more noise than friendly Frenchmen usually made on such occasions, and Quintain was in no mood to take chances. They were silhouetted sharply against the dreamy, milky, moonlit sky.

Unlucky thirteen, because Quintain had six bullets in his

revolver and, once they were gone, it would take him only seven seconds to fully reload. And he had lots of bullets, more than enough to go round, and he could see the advancing men – or most of them – very clearly, and they could not see him.

Swiftly, the millseconds fled. Swiftly, the distance between the thin, straggling line and himself was pared away. Quintain would do nothing unless compelled to, but one of the advancing men was going to stumble on him very, very soon. When that happened, Quintain would act. He would have to act. He would act fast and act finally – and act first.

And then something unexpected occurred. Something which made Quintain fractionally relax his pull on the trigger of the Webley. Out of the babble of voices approaching him, one came very clearly. The guttural, almost Germanic voice, speaking in French. "Are you sure this is where he came down?"

And that voice was answered by another. It was answered in French again, but by a voice which Quintain recognized. It was the voice of Marianne – and it made him pause.

She was with the men. He couldn't see her, but he could hear her. "He's here – he must be! And we've got to find him! He must be about here somewhere –"

Just that. That was all that Quintain heard. But it was enough to make him hesitate, despite the fact that all Fenner had inferred about Marianne was still fresh in his memory.

He could not be sure until he had said warily: "*Here I am –*" giving Marianne her first chance on enemy soil to prove herself one way or the other; hesitating on the brink of action for a tiny hiatus to see what the reaction would be.

He could do no less than that, and he did it. His voice came up out of the ground almost under the feet of the advancing men.

And it was very nearly the very last thing that Quintain ever did.

*

46

The immediate reaction was startling. Men fell over themselves in blind panic – and a gun roared.

The bullet burned Quintain – it passed that close. Then he had rolled, and come up with the eager snout of his Webley probing for a target through the milky night. He found no targets at all.

The thirteen had gone to earth – dived for the nearest available cover. Their voices were expunged from the air. With sharp, metallic snicks, Sten guns were changed from "safe" to the "fire" position.

Then Marianne's voice came again. "It *is* him! Let me go!"

There were brief sounds of a struggle. A curse.

"Let me go! It *is* him, I tell you!"

"Then let him show himself," an unmistakably Breton voice growled.

"Stand up – !" the guttural, Germanic voice took up the challenge. "Stand up and show yourself!"

The words were flung in Quintain's direction.

"It's all right, Quintain. These men are friends." Marianne's reassurance sent Quintain's eyebrows climbing. It sounded breathless. A shade off-key.

There was a smooth, flat stone beneath his hip. He moved carefully; reached for it silently. It was a large stone. He picked it up, weighed it thoughtfully in his left hand, and then tossed it forward. It hit the bushes which lay between himself and the voices. It made a sound of a man crashing through.

Instantly a revolver roared. The bullet blasted into the bushes after the stone.

Silence.

Then –

"Stop it!" Marianne cried. "Let me go! Do you know what you're doing?"

"*Ta bouche!* Shut your trap!" someone snarled roughly.

There were more sounds of struggle. More curses. Then

47

Quintain spoke. He spoke from behind the unlucky thirteen. Behind and below them. He had worked his way round them, and again he could see them quite clearly.

They were crouched in cover, but he could see them. They were above him, and their outlines were sharp against the sky.

Quintain's voice was mild as he spoke. It was almost conversational.

"If anyone moves," he said pleasantly, "I'll blow his head off. Now, Marianne –" his voice hardened "– suppose you get up very slowly and carefully and come here to me. Come with your hands empty, or I may have to kill you. Just come here – taking your time – and tell me what the hell you think you're all up to!"

CHAPTER SIX

Louis-Hercule was big and broad and built like a bull. But the slight sag to his shoulders and the streaked iron-grey in his hair made him an old one.

And, like an old bull, he was fractious, with room in his mind for only one idea at any one time. He kept twisting his heavy head on the roped skin of his thick neck and snorting in his harsh, Breton voice: "London had no need to send you! I, Louis-Hercule, bear the name of kings and of a man of power. I, Louis-Hercule, have always commanded here in Gournay en Bray!"

"But I command now," Quintain said. And it was important to say it strongly, with an air of finality, leaving no room for argument, biting the words off.

The flame in a storm lantern fluttered momentarily as it was set down in the middle of a broad, farm-house table, and the black, barred shadows swung across the thirteen faces turned inward towards his own.

"I command now," Quintain repeated. "I command until this special operation is completed."

And he had to go on. He had to say it now. He had to bring it out into the open and end it.

"Though it's small thanks to you and your men that I'm still alive – let alone able to do my job!"

"You didn't show yourself," the old man grumbled. "You could have been a Boche."

"And you – all of you –" Quintain returned sharply "– might have been a Panzer division, judging by all the noise you were making!"

"Did we frighten you then?" the old man said sneeringly. "Is that why you didn't show yourself? You were afraid!"

Quintain laughed then and laughed shortly. "Afraid?

Afraid of what? Afraid of twelve men I could – and did – run rings all around? Afraid of the Gournay Maquis?"

His contempt was cutting. Most of the pairs of eyes turned towards his own glittered angrily. Louis-Hercule's own face darkened with furious blood. The old bull began to speak thickly. Quintain silenced him with a swift, commanding motion of his hand.

"What was there to be afraid of? You saw what use your guns were to you! Outnumbered twelve to one, with luck I could have killed all of you! You ought to go down on your knees and thank the good God that I wasn't a German! Afraid –?" He laughed again, and then stopped abruptly. "But before I am finished with you, I promise you, I will make the Gournay en Bray Maquis into somethng that men *will* be afraid of!"

He had them now. He had their unwilling, grudging attention, and he had all of it. His personality dominated the room.

He said harshly: "And who fired at me? Which one of you fired at me?"

Sulkily, the youngest member of the group, a blond, tousle-haired young man in his late teens, acknowledged the eyes which reluctantly moved his way.

"I did," he said. And his voice was the gutturally Germanic one that Quintain had heard earlier.

"Bravo!" Quintain said ironically. "And if I'd shown myself as you demanded of me, you'd have shot me dead, eh? Bravo!"

Then his voice hardened. "Your name?"

"Paul –"

"You, Paul, have some explaining to do," Quintain told him bleakly. "Why did you fire at me? You were expecting a friend, not an enemy, and yet you opened fire without warning – and without cause! You very nearly did a good night's work for the Boche. Why?"

Then the thing which really worried Quintain – the skulking thought which had been suppressed so long and could be quieted no longer — came out sharply: "Perhaps that's what you wanted to do — a good night's work for the Hun! Perhaps that's what was in your mind!"

The young man's blazing, furious denial told Quintain nothing. It was neither more, nor less, than he had expected. The simmering, bitter-mouthed explanation which followed was a repetition of Louis-Hercule's own grumbling complaint. "You didn't show yourself. You could have been a Boche . . ."

Somehow from Louis-Hercule, the old bull, it was an acceptable explanation. From the young, yellow-haired Paul, however, it was not.

Louis-Hercule was old and past his prime, and Quintain thought that the man himself knew it. He had been providing an excuse, not for a series of positive actions, but for his inability to lead and control men.

In effect, Louis-Hercule had been denying that inability by implying that what had been done had been at his instigation — which Quintain doubted. He was more inclined to believe that Louis-Hercule, the man who had always led in the Gournay en Bray Maquis, had simply lost his grip on the men he commanded. Though the old bull would never admit it.

All this was understandable behaviour in a man who, for thirty years, had been caught up in a legend, Quintain thought. He knew Louis-Hercule's personal history.

The old bull had been one of Petain's heroes at Verdun in the Great War, three times decorated, and in the peace which had followed he had come to settle in Gournay en Bray, there to be flattered as the big fish in the small pond always is.

He had been looked up to as a patriot and a Boche-killer, and his opinions had been solicited on every question of the day, moral, military, and political, as a matter of course.

Naturally, he had always led in Gournay en Bray! Sipping

his wine at a crowded table on the pavement opposite the *Hotel de Ville* he had been the natural leader. And, of course, he couldn't admit his inability to lead now.

All this was understandable. Everything Louis-Hercule had done and said was understandable. But all that young Paul had done and said was not.

And Marianne's own heated intervention to say that she knew and trusted Paul from her previous service with this Maquis, and that Quintain's insinuations were impossible and unthinkable, served only to make Quintain more wary and doubtful than ever.

In view of all of Fenner's remarks, Marianne was cast in the role of the Devil's Advocate. Nothing more; nothing less.

*

Now they were talking together, Marianne and young Paul, talking in low, guarded voices in a shadowed corner of the farmhouse kitchen as Quintain, at the table, pushed a long finger across a map and explained the preliminaries of the special operation to Louis-Hercule for a second time, at the old Frenchman's own request.

Quintain was being just as careful on this second occasion, as on the first, to speak in very general terms.

High-explosive had to be collected from points A, B, and C. – his forefinger touched the map here, here, and here. *After that, a target of supreme military importance would be blown up* . . .

However, where precisely the target was, and what it was, and who would actually engineer its destruction, Quintain carefully neglected to say.

He was remembering everything that Fenner had told him, and being very careful. His voice went on, his hands moved, and all the while Louis-Hercule's face grew darker and darker . . .

All of the other members of the Maquis had listened to

Quintain's first outline of the special operation, and now most of them had gone. They had left the farmhouse, dispersed for what remained of the night, taking the bulk of the arms and equipment dropped in the parachutage with them. All these supplies would be well hidden, in half-a-dozen caches scattered across the countryside, before the first light of dawn.

Only two canisters remained, and these contained a quantity of high explosive. Necessarily, for safety's sake, it was a small quantity in relation to the canister's size and weight. Two *maquisards* besides Louis-Hercule and young Paul remained – Guillaume and Rene.

Guillaume was long and lean with the deep-wrinkled, tanned-leather face and clear, almost translucent eyes of a fisherman. He was in his mid-forties. The other man, Rene, was younger, and smaller, and smoother, and darker. He was carefully dressed, almost dapper. His skin was sallow, like that of a Corsican. At this moment, Guillaume was outside the farmhouse, keeping watch, and Rene sat on the floor with his back to a wall, his Sten gun propped up beside him, and his head slumped forward across folded arms. He was dozing fitfully until it was his turn to mount guard.

At the table Quintain straightened up. He was very tired. He had been up for most of the previous night. There had been a thousand-and-one details to check and things to see to. Now, with the yellow light from the lantern full on his face, lines of fatigue showed around his mouth and his eyes. He said to Louis-Hercule: "That's it, then. That's the operation in outline. That's what we've got to do – "

And then he waited.

He pushed the maps with his fingers, and let them roll. He knew what was coming next – what was bound to come next. He waited for it.

He knew why Louis-Hercule had asked for a repetition of the briefing he had given the men of the Maquis. He knew why he had been asked for a second explanation.

53

The old bull's face was darker than ever. He said ominously to Quintain: "And is this all you are going to tell me?"

"It's all I can tell you," said Quintain quietly, and the long-awaited storm broke.

"So – we go here, we go there, we do this, we do that – we risk our lives and the life of every member of our families – and all the time we know nothing, or next to nothing!"

Precipitating the old man's anger, bringing it on – the more quickly roused, the more quickly over – Quintain said mildly: "What exactly is it that worries you, Louis-Hercule? No other member of your Maquis has complained – "

"No-one else has complained – ? Is that what you say to *me*? I, Louis-Hercule, who bear the name of kings and who used to lead here! Is this what long, hard years of devotion to France has brought me? An answer like that? Am I, Louis-Hercule, three times decorated, ten times wounded killing the Boche, am I to be lumped with the rest?"

The angry Frenchman's voice was almost a bellow.

"No-one else here has complained, so I must be silent, too, eh? We are all to be puppets on strings – children not to be trusted – "

Quintain shrugged. "I am sorry – "

"You are sorry! Aren't we entitled to know what we are doing, and why? Aren't I, at least, entitled to know? These are my men! This is my Maquis! I raised it from nothing! From nothing, I tell you! And, until now, I have led it – "

"I still cannot say more than I have said, Louis-Hercule."

"These are my men! You are using them! By any standard, I have a right – "

"They are France's men," Quintain said, interrupting. "They are men of Free France. They are not my men, nor yours."

Guillaume came in, and Rene roused himself and went out, and young Paul and Marianne sat quietly listening in

54

the corner, and the storm raged on around the lantern set on the table in the middle of the farmhouse kitchen.

"I led here until you came! For a 'Special Operation' – " Louis-Hercule uttered the words with scathing sarcasm " – a new leader is sent from London! A Frenchman to lead Frenchmen? Oh, no! An Englishman. Until you came, I led. I was a man – an important man – before you were whelped. And now I am treated like a child!"

But the storm was blowing itself out. Quintain remained unmoved and unmoving. He refused to compromise. The old man's thunder fell into a grumble which finally muttered away into silence.

The night passed.

Then the false dawn was grey in the east. A young cockerel, destined soon for the pot, stretched its neck, deceived, and crowed. In the farmyard, by a gateway on to a track across the fields, the small and sallow Rene yawned and spat and scratched himself, swung the sling of his Sten gun over his shoulder, and yawned again.

Far off, in London, at Admiral Lord Louis Mountbatten's Combined Operations' Headquarters, despatch riders came and went endlessly throughout the night and into the dawn. Messages were received and sent and, all the while – as Rene yawned, and Louis-Hercule grumbled, and Quintain set up his portable radio transmitter in a small room under the eaves of the farmhouse and tapped out his first message to Fenner – the planning, the preparations, the checking and cross-checking continued in London.

It continued as German grenadiers, pacing the western wall of the fortress of Europe, gazed seaward in the dawn and wondered if the mad Englanders would really come. It continued as Richard Quintain's first signal was quickly received and swiftly decoded and urgently acknowledged and as, in orderly rooms and cramped company offices and makeshift headquarters throughout the south of England, blackout shutters were lifted down from windows and the new day's first strong, harsh brew of tea appeared, thick with "scrounged" condensed milk and scalding hot, to revive men and officers who had been working over maps and battle-plans the whole night through.

It continued in the dawn and in the day – the day which was Monday, the seventeenth of August, nineteen forty-two.

From Pershore, in Worcestershire, aerial reconnaissance aircraft went out, sweeping low over the English country-side, scudding at zero feet across the Channel, banking and climbing swiftly over the harbour entrance to Dieppe.

Dieppe . . . On that day this was a place-name written and spoken again and again. It was a name which loomed larger and larger in men's thoughts and calculations. It dominated their minds.*

It was a name spoken apprehensively; spoken positively; spoken with thin, inner and hidden fear making the mouth dry. It was a name spoken – only sometimes – confidently; roundly, like a sergeant-major's curse.

Dieppe . . .

The aerial reconnaissance aircraft came back with photo-graphs which seemed to complete the Combined Operations' picture of the port's defences. The last pieces fell into place in the operational jig-saw. The suspected presence of pill-boxes concealed in the caves of the Eastern headland was confirmed. Tanks were revealed encased in concrete walls at the end of the Western breakwater.

*In Egypt, at 8th Army Headquarters, General Montgomery couldn't help thinking about it.

Dieppe.

It was no longer his pigeon. Not his responsibility any more. He had been posted out here to command the 8th Army and to knock the Germans for six in North Africa. France was far, far away. But he couldn't ignore his uneasiness.

It persisted.

As soon as he'd known that the-raid-that-never-was had been put back on operational footing again, he had written to General Paget, Commander-in-Chief Home Forces: "If they want to do something on the Continent, let them choose another target than Dieppe."

But no-one had listened.

56

At ten o'clock that morning, the preliminary order of assault was issued. Operation Jubilee was confirmed for nautical twilight on the morning of the nineteenth of August – now less than forty-eight hours away.

Dieppe . . .

Broad bars of sunlight shafted into the vast room in Kensington's Natural History Museum which Felix Fenner had commandeered as his office. It was a room big enough to house a mammoth. In fact, at one time, it had. But now, at this moment, it contained only Felix Fenner himself.

He sat, half-swallowed by the big chair, motionless, brooding over a broad desk laden with papers and dusted with the fine ash of innumerable cigarettes. Two telephones, one black and one red, stood squat and silent before him. Then, at eleven o'clock precisely, the red telephone began to ring.

It rang once, and once only, and then Fenner's thin, skeletal hand fastened on it. And Fenner uttered only one word as his long forefinger plunged down on the scrambler button. One word which, for all its brevity, still managed – somehow – to carry more than its full weight of ominous foreboding.

"*Yes . . .?*"

"It's on. Definitely on!"

The voice which reached Fenner was clipped and urgent. It was also jubilant. "The first waves go in at five o'clock on Wednesday morning. And I've got permission to go in with them!"

Fenner tugged his small beard sourly as he listened. *You poor fool,* he thought. *You poor fool. You still think that war is a game, don't you? You've got permission to go – perhaps to your death – and you're as pleased as if you were a schoolboy again and chosen to captain the First Eleven!*

But he said none of these things, only thought them. He said only: "Congratulations, sir," and saw the wall-clock and the calendar below it. Five o'clock on Wednesday morning – forty-two hours away.

"You've got all your plans made?" The man on the other end of the line was a brigadier, and now he spoke tersely. "I'm more than usually interested in 'em now – as you can imagine. Those E-boat pens – "

"Will be destroyed on schedule," Fenner said, and made his voice confident.

The E-boat pens had to be destroyed on schedule! Richard Quintain had to see to it that they were.

Men's lives depended upon it. Perhaps a lot of men's lives. And perhaps more than men's lives – Fenner couldn't help thinking.

He'd never been happy about this operation. He couldn't stop himself from anticipating the worst.*

It might be that it wouldn't be the success that the Combined Operations Planning Staff hoped for. It might be that only Richard Quintain and a handful of Frenchmen would stand between an orderly withdrawal from Dieppe's

*Opening paragraphs of the German —
ORDER OF THE DAY

G.OC. 15th Army   Army H.Q. 10–8–42

Information which has reached us makes it quite clear that the Anglo-Americans will be forced to undertake some operation in the West in the very near future. They must do something:

(a) in order to keep their Russian allies fighting;
(b) for home front reasons.

I have repeatedly brought this to the attention of the troops, and I ask that my orders on this matter be constantly kept before them so that the idea sinks in thoroughly, and they expect nothing else.

(order signed by
Colonel-General HAASE,
General Officer Commanding
15th Army)

In Dieppe, the German troops were in the highest state of readiness. In fact, all ranks were now beginning to get rather bored with the whole business, and rather tired of the constant drilling and training which had reached fever pitch during the past few months. A great deal of work had been done to improve the fortifications in and around the town. And work would still be in progress on these defences until – significantly – August 18th.

beaches at the operation's end and the fiasco of a rout more crippling in its consequences to men and morale than anything ever experienced before. More damaging even than Dunkirk had been.

The red phone went back on its rest, and the brigadier was left to his jubilation, and Fenner to his nagging, worrying doubts. At Combined Operations Headquarters, Admiral Lord Louis Mountbatten ordered a car. He drove quickly to the headquarters of Number Eleven Group Fighter Command for one last conference with Lieutenant-General Crerar and Air-Vice-Marshal Leigh Mallory. The detailed maps of the whole operation were before them.

From that time on, until the end of Operation Jubilee, Number Eleven Group Headquarters would be Mountbatten's own headquarters, too. From there, through radio contact with the Force Commanders, he would be able to keep a finger on the pulse of events from the very first moment of assault.

Major-General Roberts was in command of the Military Force. Air Commodore Cole was Air Liaison Officer Afloat. Captain Hughes-Hallett was in command of the Naval Force.

The dispositions were made, the plans long since finalised. After the last conference, all that remained left to do was to wait.

The weather forecast predicted a smooth sea, a fine day for the assault, and no swell.

Throughout Southern England, men and munitions of war were nearing the ports of embarkation. If they didn't already know it, men were being told their target – *Dieppe*.

Across the narrow sea which separated the United Kingdom from Hitler's fortress of Europe, Richard Quintain – the man on whom Felix Fenner was certain so much depended – was already moving into action.

*

The battered old van rattled loudly as it bucked over the fields of Northern France in the early morning.

It was an ancient blue-grey Renault which had been converted to run on charcoal and woodchips instead of petrol. It had a smoking upright boiler bolted on to the running board beside the driver's cab, and it snorted and snuffled and sneezed as it approached the farmhouse some few kilometres south of Gournay en Bray.

Outside the open door of the farmhouse, the young, blond, and almost Germanic *maquisard* known as Paul stood stubbing the dirt with his toe and glowering impartially at the approaching Renault van and at Richard Quintain. His guttural voice was raised harshly. "I, for one, don't like it! I still don't like it!"

Quintain had not long told his companions that the van would be coming. He had not long told them what the van would be bringing. He had been careful to hold back the information until the very last possible moment before the van actually appeared.

Now, in the background, Louis-Hercule moved his massive head and grunted from his broad chest: "It is not what *you* like that counts, Paul! If this is necessary for the sake of France, then we will do it!"

Quintain looked at the old bull of a man, very surprised. He had not expected such outright support for his plans from this quarter. Nor had young Paul expected the rebuke. Angrily, he swung away.

And thoughtfully, grizzled head on chest, Louis-Hercule watched him round a corner of the farmhouse and pass out of sight. Then the old bull sucked at his teeth, made to say something, and then changed his mind. Instead, he shifted his feet, planting them wide apart, and fixed his eyes on the approaching blue-grey Renault van. Casually he remarked: "Paul comes from Alsace you know . . ."

Interestedly he regarded the Renault as it rattled nearer.

"I know that now," Quintain said. "But at first his accent had me worried."

"In the dark, you mean. When you parachuted down into the field . . . yes. His accent is so like a German's . . ."

Louis-Hercule narrowed his eyes and spat in the dirt. Then he changed the subject abruptly. He nodded in the direction of the approaching van. "Not pretty, is it? And it sounds as if it's on its last legs. But I know these converted Renaults. They look terrible and the sound worse – fit only for the scrapyard – but they can go. Given half a chance they'll show many a Mercedes a clean pair of heels . . ."

Again he spat.

"I don't know what young Paul is worried about!"

Quintain did and that was the trouble. He understood full well what worried the tall, blond Alsatian, and there was absolutely nothing he could do about it. The idea of riding around the roads of Occupied France with an ever-mounting load of high-explosives and detonators behind him – and more than a chance of meeting a German patrol on the way – was what was worrying Paul. Who could find fault with that?

"If we were to meet a patrol, we'd be done for!" Paul had exclaimed angrily. "What could we do if we met a patrol? Stop, and let the Germans search the van? It'd be a firing squad for all of us! Try and make a break for it – with high-explosive and detonators at our backs?" His mouth had twisted sourly. "It would be madness. It *is* madness! The first bullet will see us all blown to glory!"

But the explosive had to be moved somehow. It had to be delivered within the next thirty-six hours. There was little time – hardly any – and more explosive had to be collected along the way.

"But why do we have to do it like this?" Paul had demanded, and he had regarded Quintain suspiciously, as though this plan could only be the result of some freakish whim on the Englishman's part. "We've never done it this way before."

Could Quintain point out that an E-boat base had never been utterly destroyed before by the Maquis? Could he point out that no operation of this size had ever been attempted before by any unit of the French Resistance? He could not.

He had told Louis-Hercule and his men only that 'something vital to the enemy' had to be destroyed. He had not told them what that 'something' was. He could not do so now.

"Why –" young Paul had demanded "– do we have to move explosive and detonators over the roads when the R.A.F. can move them more quickly and easily across the sky? We can have them dropped wherever we want them. The R.A.F. will drop all we need . . ."

Could Quintain answer that, to begin with, there was no time for the R.A.F. to drop all the explosive required? Could he go on to say that, even if the time-factor didn't exist, the high-explosive and detonators could be dropped no nearer the operation's target than they already were?

No. All we could do was to cut short all argument abruptly. He declared flatly: "It's not convenient," and left Paul glowering and dissatisfied. Without giving a hint of the operation's target he could say no more.

He certainly could not explain to the young Alsatian that the "something" which had to be destroyed was an integral part of the heavily-defended German West Wall – an impossible place for a parachutage. He could not tell him that without telling him everything.

The way Quintain planned to fulfil his assignment was the only way. The Renault was bringing explosives from Amiens, to which would be added the contents of the two canisters in the farmhouse kitchen.

The battered old van was then going on to Rouen, where more explosives and detonators would be collected, and from there to Yvetot, in a semi-circular sweep across the countryside, where the last consignment would be picked up.

The final rendezvous was to be kept between Dieppe and Treport, where all the explosives and detonators Quintain had collected would – at the very last moment – be handed over to the men who would actually use them.

All this had been arranged before Quintain and Marianne had even left England, and a timetable had been worked out. The timetable kept the explosives in Quintain's hands and under his control until the last possible moment. This was necessary, for there were few places of concealment in the enemy-infested environs of the West Wall.

The men who would use the explosives had nowhere to hide them. Therefore, Quintain must only deliver them immediately before they were to be used.

But could he explain all this to anybody?

The way Quintain planned to fulfil this assignment was was the only way possible, but he could not make the Frenchmen see this without inviting further questions.

And further questions were the very last things that he wanted. For they would, necessarily, be questions he could not permit himself to answer.

CHAPTER SEVEN

THE blue-grey Renault van bounced over the last few deep ruts into the farmyard. Quintain and Louis-Hercule went to meet it, and Paul reappeared with Marianne behind him. The Renault lurched to a halt.

"A brute," the driver said cheerfully, clambering down from his cab. And, just as cheerfully, he gave the upright boiler a kick as he passed it.

He was a round, fat fellow encircled with a deep-biting leather belt which unsuccessfully attempted to separate his sagging chest from his bulging stomach.

He swung off the jacket draped around his shoulders and flung it back into the cab. His bare forearms were muscular and matted with long, curling black hair. He pushed a battered blue cap on to the back of his head and wiped his nose with the back of a broad hand. It was the same hand which he thrust forward immediately afterwards.

"Alphonse," he said, introducing himself. "And you are –?"

"Louis-Hercule, *le patron*, and –"

"The Englishman. *Boné*" Alphonse seized them, one after the other, by the hand.

Then: "The soup's in the back," he said, jerking his head towards the old Renault van. "There's more to be loaded, and then –?"

"Then Rouen," Quintain said, and Alphonse sucked in his breath sharply and held it there for a second. "Rouen ...?"

He wiped his nose again. Then he said, almost apologetically: "The Boches are out on the roads –"

"Of course they're out on the roads!" the young Paul put

in explosively. "And before we get anywhere near Rouen, we'll be stopped!"

Alphonse's small eyes slid sideways to fasten on the tall, blond young man. One of his eyebrows went up interrogatively. "Paul," Louis-Hercule said briefly. "The youngest of my group."

"Hmph!" Alphonse grunted. And Paul flared: "Is that a crime?"

Alphonse didn't answer. He just let his eyes travel back to rest on Quintain's face, and he waited. His whole attitude said that he, for one, knew who was making the decisions and giving the orders here in Gournay en Bray at this moment.

He had made his point about the Germans being out on the roads, and he was content to wait. He put himself completely in Quintain's hands as the leader of his *Maquis*, an ex-Inspector of the Surete Nationale, had told him he should do.

"My *patron* sends his best wishes," he said. "He would have liked to have come himself."

And Quintain nodded, smiling, having heard all about Alphonse's leader from Felix Fenner. "A devil, that man. A devil incarnate where the Huns are concerned . . ."

Then he moved.

"We carry on as planned," Quintain said, and there was nothing else he could say. His way was the only way, the refrain was repeated.

Paul snorted his disgust. Louis-Hercule, Rene and Alphonse went with Quintain to empty the canisters in the farmhouse kitchen and load up the Renault.

*

"And now where the devil has he got to?" Louis-Hercule growled.

The high-explosive and detonators were loaded and the

65

men, with Marianne, stood around the van. But of Paul there was no sign.

"Where has he got to? He knew we were all going to Rouen together."

Above a small wood some distance away from the farm-house, birds wheeled in sudden flight. One broke free of the rest, skidded round in a wide turn, and headed south.

A pigeon? Quintain wondered, and frowned. It was hard to tell at that distance.

"Where *is* he?" Louis-Hercule growled again.

Guillaume shrugged his shoulders. His weather-beaten, fisherman's face was blank. "I wasn't here."

Marianne, under Quintain's eye, said hurriedly: "I thought he went back into the house for something . . ." Her voice tailed off.

Alphonse said carefully, expressionlessly: "It seemed to me he was sure there would be trouble along the way." He moved his shoulders delicately. "Perhaps . . ."

Louis-Hercule broke in abruptly. "Whatever young Paul may be, he's not a coward!"

Alphonse moved his shoulders again and fell silent. Quintain, his eyes on the little wood beyond the farmhouse, frowned again. "Well, we can't wait –"

Then came a distraction. A sudden exclamation from Louis-Hercule brought all their heads around sharply. Someone was plunging and bucking along on a bicycle over the fields. Someone who waved frantically and shouted.

"But that's Armand, from Rouen!" Louis-Hercule thrust forward solidly to the farmyard gate. "That's who it is – Armand! Why has he come here? What's happened?"

They were soon to know.

Armand, thin-faced, angular and worried-looking, shout-ed his news before he reached them.

The leader of the Maquis in Rouen had been taken by the Germans not two hours before. He had been taken alive – they all knew what that meant.

"He'll talk. The Gestapo will make him talk."

"The head of the Gestapo in Rouen is a woman," Alphonse got out, dry-mouthed. "I have heard –"

"She is a bitch. A bitch from hell, that one!" Louis-Hercule declared passionately. "She questions men herself. She is clever –"

"Quiet!" Quintain snapped, and they stared at him. But how could he think with so much noise all around him?

He said abruptly to Louis-Hercule: "You have a motor-cycle here?" He had seen it.

"It belongs to young Paul. Where *is* Paul –?" Louis-Hercule started to say, and then stopped. The tall, young Alsatian had rejoined them silently.

"And where have you been?" Head lowered, Louis-Hercule glowered at him.

"I –"

"Never mind," Quintain put in. "Time for that later. Your motor-cycle, Paul –"

"What about it?"

"Armand wants to borrow it."

"I *do* –?"

"If the leader of your Maquis is in the hands of the Germans," Quintain said, "all the arrangements which were made with him on my behalf will have to be changed. We are coming to Rouen to pick up explosives. Where will they be cached?"

"The caches will have to be changed too –"

"I hope so," said Quintain. "Armand, you'd better get back to Rouen. Lend him that motor-cycle of yours, Paul."

The Alsatian seemed unwilling.

"Lend it to him," Louis-Hercule growled.

"But if the Germans –"

"The Germans are just as likely to get it here as anywhere else. Lend it to him."

With very bad grace, Paul consented.

"Then, Armand, tell your comrades in Rouen that we'll meet them in – how long, Alphonse? You know your Renault."

"How long to get from here to Rouen? An hour. Ninety minutes at the most."

"Say two hours," Quintain amended. He fixed his eyes on Armand. "Tell your friends we'll meet them in two hours from now. And where, Marianne? You know Rouen. Somewhere where we can talk with no danger of being overheard. A place no Germans frequent for choice."

"The Cafe de Deux Magots should be safe enough at this time," Marianne said.

She said it emotionally. Flatly.

Paul looked at her quickly, and she glanced away again.

*

It was an open road; a fine road; an empty road.

It was straight and open and empty half the way to Rouen.

The sun was high and the day was hot and the blue-grey Renault van moved at a cautious speed.

Not too slowly it went; not too fast. Alphonse the driver, was mindful of his load of high-explosive, and he was also giving himself ample time to turn off the road entirely on to one of the innumerable cart-tracks should any German patrol come swinging out of the heat-hazed distance ahead.

Alphonse sang as he drove. Pushing his battered cap on to the back of his oily black hair, he sang in a high, cracked Italianate tenor. He was happy.

Beside him, in the cab, his knee nudging his Sten gun, the short and swarthy Rene winced visibly at some of Alphonse's over-sustained top notes.

In the body of the van behind them, separated from the cab by only a thin plywood partition, Quintain and Louis-Hercule swayed knee to knee with Guillaume and Marianne and Paul. Carefully wedged into place all around them were small cylinders of high-explosive.

The atmosphere in the body of the van was close and airless. Guillaume, his fisherman's face relaxed, somehow managed to sleep unmoving. Louis-Hercule broke the silence to speak occasionally to Quintain, and then only to remark on some landmark seen through the van's side windows, and confirm that they were making good time.

Now and again, every so often, Quintain moved his head look through the small pane of dusty glass set in the rear to wall of the driver's cab. Looking forward over the shoulders of Rene and Alphonse and across the blunt snout of Rene's Sten gun he could see the road unwinding as the Renault rattled and swayed on.

He could also see, as a ghost reflection in the glass, that Marianne regarded him covertly whenever his back was turned, looking at him strangely and speaking in a guarded undertone to Paul.

The van drove on, and the road ahead was as empty as ever. Half a mile away, a grove of poplars skirted it on the right-hand side. A small cloud crossed the sun . . .

A small cloud crossed the sun, and the light died. The interior of the van was dark now. The road ahead, as Quintain scanned it, was momentarily grey and rather menacing.

It seemed a little too empty, he thought a trifle uneasily. Everything was running too smoothly . . .

A little wind, blowing up out of nowhere, made the poplars move as the blue-grey van drew nearer.

Alphonse was still singing, but not as loudly as before. Rene was moving restlessly beside him. Guillaume was awake . . .

And then it happened.

It happened swiftly and methodically. So swiftly and methodically that Quintain, afterwards, was to be quite sure that it had been thoroughly planned.

The unknown traitor had added this to his – or her – treachery.

As the Renault drew level with the grove of poplars, the sun blazed out from behind its cloud. Simultaneously, German soldiers spilled out of cover and across the road.

There were ten of them – nine men and an officer. They blocked the road both in front of the Renault and behind it. Their machine carbines were levelled. In the middle of the road, the officer, tall and young, flung up his hand. "*Halte!*"

What happened next happened with frightening speed.

Rene tried to get his Sten gun up, but was stopped by a pistol thrust against the side of his neck. One of the Germans had jumped on to the running board of the truck.

"*Halte-oder wir schiesen! Halt, or we fire!*"

Then –

"Down!" Alphonse yelled and accelerated. He put the Renault straight at the German officer in the middle of the road. But the next instant Alphonse was dead. He died as the corporal hanging on to the running board fired.

Rene grabbed for the wheel. There were explosives behind him – enough to blow everyone to glory. He grabbed for the wheel, now slippery with Alphonse's blood, and as he did so the German corporal hanging on to the running board slammed his smoking pistol hard under his ear.

"*Brake!*" the German shouted.

The van lurched to a halt only inches away from the tall officer in the middle of the road. The officer had disdained to move. The other soldiers closed in. They surrounded the van, machine carbines held at the ready. They were very wary.

"*Down!*" the corporal said above and behind the pistol held at Rene's head. The swarthy Frenchman, sweat beading his face, had to push Alphonse's slack body off himself before he could obey.

He got down slowly. As slowly as he dared. His fingertips,

70

blood-stained and wet, were within millimetres of the Sten gun as he backed out of the cab.

Dare he reach for it? Dare he try to take it? One false move and he would die –

The young officer stalked forward and hammered on the side of the van. "All out! *Hände hoch!* All out with your hands up! *Raus!* All out!"

The machine-carbines came closer, still ringing the Renault round, making escape impossible.

"All out! All out!" the officer repeated, and blows fell again upon the side of the van.

"All out!"

And he gave the order first in French – *and then in English.*

CHAPTER EIGHT

ALONG the South Coast of England, at Newhaven, Shoreham, Southampton and Portsmouth, a fleet of two hundred and fifty-two little ships was being made in all respects ready for sea.

In the early afternoon of that burning, airless Monday they were loading ammunition.

At Biggin Hill, at Kenley, at Northolt, at Tangmere, at West Malling, Debden, Ford, Hornchurch, North Weald and half-a-dozen other airfields, fighters and bombers were being worked over by maintenance teams which laboured, and would labour, all the way round the clock.

At Petworth in Sussex, and in a score of tented camps like it, Canadians were writing home – the last letter: *"Dear Mom and Dad . . ."*

They lifted pens from paper. They knew where they were going, but they couldn't put it on paper. And would this be their last letter home . . . ever? Their reason told them that on the day after the morrow they might well be dead, but that stubborn unwillingness in men to admit of anything but personal immortality still held them prisoner.

So they wrote this last letter as an ordinary one – but an extra one. Or they wrote it as a last one – just in case – not believing what they wrote.

"Dear Mom and Dad . . ."

Their eyes, smoky with memories, peered out across the oceans. They saw again the cold streets of the Canadian cities; cold, not from lack of sun or heat, but in some strange way, some indefinable way, cold from lack of human warmth.

A Canadian city does not feel like home to anyone. It is

a place to be; a place to eat, and sleep, and occasionally drink. It is a place to live in, work in and make love in – but it is not home.

Yet, for many of these men; for many of the five thousand Canadian officers and men who would assault Dieppe, the cities were the only homes they knew.

The others were luckier. The others who had not come from the indefinably cold cities, but from the plains. From the plains and the lakes and the forests thick with pine and spruce and canoe birch; from the song of the saw and the thud of the axe and the snort of the motorized plough carving up the great fallow places. These were the lucky ones.

In memory, the endless silence of the plains and the forests – that silence which is not a silence – contained and comforted them. It wrapped them round about.

The wild duck wheeled over the lakes in raucous flight; the sun dappled the floor of the great forest; water tossed itself, ice-cold and crystal-clear down clefts in rocks a hundred feet deep and already old when Montcalm still held the Heights of Abraham and Quebec was little more than a fortified village.

What could they say?

The officers appointed to censor the mail moved restlessly between the row of tents. There was so much to do, and so little time. They were impatient.

In London, in a vast, echoing hall of an office carved out of one of the galleries in the Natural History Museum, a small bearded man silenced a clamorous crimson telephone for the tenth time that day. The bearded man's calm voice spoke.

"Yes, yes; everything's under control. Nothing to worry about. Yes, yes, the E-boats will be taken care of. Yes, you can depend on that. There's absolutely nothing to worry about . . . no, not a thing."

Nothing to worry about – and, in France, eight kilometres short of the city of Rouen, German soldiers ringed the blue-grey Renault van.

Machine-carbines were rock-steady in their hands as their young, tall officer hit the side of the van sharply.

"All out! All out! *Raus!*"

*

Inside the body of the blue-grey van, there was a split second's silence during which nothing happened, and time stood still.

Then everything shifted out of focus. Everything happened at once. Everybody moved at once.

The German officer's blows fell on the side of the van. There was a harsh repetition of the command to come out. With a savage rattle, the machine-carbines of the German soldiers ringing the van slammed out of the safe and into the fire position.

Paul, his eyes haunted, darted a glance from Quintain to the stacked containers of explosive and detonators. His lips moved, but no words came. Louis-Hercule was hunched forward. He looked ill. His face was suddenly that of an old, old man.

"*Oh, mon Dieu!*"

A blur of movement, and the young Paul was up on his feet. Guillaume was saying, like a man suddenly awakened from sleep: "Without all that high-explosive we'd have stood a chance –"

Louis-Hercule's head came up. With a great effort, his massive shoulders squared. "We could still take the swine with us! We could still all go together –"

Then his voice rose high. "What are you doing? Where are you going?"

Wordlessly, his face ashen, Paul was blundering towards the rear door of the van. He was opening it.

74

"Coward!" bellowed Louis-Hercule.

It was in the same moment that Quintain saw the trap-door in the van's floor.

It was only a small trapdoor, let into the floor midway along the body of the van. An inspection trap, little more. But Quintain had pulled it up and out of the way before Paul had got the rear door open, and Guillaume, divining what was in his mind, cocked his Sten and thrust it at the Englishman all in one movement.

"Here!"

Quintain slammed the Sten bodily through the opening, swung it horizontal to the road but upside down, and fired.

The gun leapt in his hands. He almost dropped it. He swung it like a scythe, and like a scythe it cut the enemy down. Soft-nosed bullets slammed into legs and knees and thighs. One of the van's tyres was shot through. The vehicle lurched sickeningly and Paul, losing his balance in the open doorway, was thrown into the road.

Rene, by the side of the van, heard the revolver held behind him explode. He felt the wind of the bullet, and leapt for the safety of the running board. In the same moment he had his Sten in his hands, and it was bucking and twisting as, sweat streaming into his eyes, he bared his teeth and swore above it.

The windscreen of the van went out in a hail of shattered glass. The German officer, racing for cover, was cut down before he'd gone three yards. A German soldier, crippled, his knees splintered, screamed and got his carbine to his shoulder and went on screaming as he fired. His bullets ploughed into the driver's cab and Rene felt warm blood run down his face.

Then Guillaume was out on the road, a pistol in his hand, and his fisherman's eyes were slate-grey as he fired and fired again. .

There was a sudden silence. Quiet came rushing into vacuum left after the fury of battle had gone. German

75

soldiers sprawled over the road in attitudes of death. The young officer lay on his face and – ridiculously – at attention.

Alphonse, the driver, sprawled half-in and half-out of the cab of the van, his flesh drained of blood, very waxen, almost yellow, his eyes wide open and staring.

Quintain let the Sten gun drop into the road beneath the van. He stood upright inside it. He felt tiredness come upon him. The tiredness which comes to all men after killing.

He got out of the back of the van and stood in the road.

Carefully, Louis-Hercule followed him down. The old man was shaking. Paul got to his feet. His face was wet with sweat. There was a ragged tear in one sleeve of the jacket he wore. He seemed to have been hit. Bright drops of blood fell from his fingertips.

"One of my bullets," Quintain said. "I'm sorry."

Paul found his voice as, with a trembling hand, he probed the ragged tear in his sleeve. "It is nothing."

Quintain stood quite still and quite silent a moment, and then he began to move. He went down the road and stood over the young German officer. He turned him over onto his back.

The man was quite dead. He looked pathetically young. Then Quintain, with the sudden burning sensation of eyes upon him, looked sharply up. Astonished, he found himself gazing into the face of a German soldier. An unarmed German soldier who was cowering in the undergrowth by the edge of the road, not more than six feet away.

Quintain opened his mouth to speak. "*Kamaradé*" the German soldier cried, and flung himself forward, empty-handed and unarmed.

And then he stopped.

The young maquisard called Paul was upon him. And he started to say something just as Paul reached him, but the words died in his throat. They died as Paul emptied a heavy revolver into his head at point-blank range.

The soldier was battered backwards by bullets. He sprawled in his blood and his brains. Quintain's lips were thin and white. "Did you need to do that?"

His voice was terribly angry.

"The only good Boche is a dead one!" Paul told him, and kicked the still-warm corpse.

"Get away from him!" Quintain's eyes blazed with fury. Then, slowly, he bent down over the dead German officer again as, after a moment's hesitation, Paul slowly withdrew.

And then, suddenly, the German officer's papers in his hands, Quintain was jerked upright yet again as another shot smashed out behind him. He wheeled around to see that one of the dead German soldiers in the road had come to life again – only to die once more.

The man had reached his machine-carbine, only millimetres away from his outstretched hands when he had fallen. He had reached his machine-carbine and his finger had been on the trigger; the gun pointed unwaveringly at Quintain.

Near him stood Marianne, pale-faced, a pistol still smoking in her grasp.

"I had to kill him," she got out. "He . . . he would have killed *you*."

CHAPTER NINE

THROUGH the golden August afternoon, German soldiers sauntered the length of Rouen's wide, white *Rue de la Republique*.

Some walked in pairs or in groups. Others walked singly. Some ambled along with gaily-dressed French girls at their side. All walked idly and easily, enjoying the sunshine and taking their ease. They were all men who were either on leave or off duty. They were all very much at home here.

Along the broad street they went, a casually drifting human tide, past the great Gothic eastern aspect of the cathedral, mingling lazily with the shopping crowds, jingling coins in their pockets. Along the broad *Rue de la Republique* they went to the *Quai de Paris* and the shimmering golden sparkle of the swiftly-flowing River Seine.

Quintain thought it was an easy scene to watch. It was the kind of scene one could have witnessed in any leave town in almost any country in this third year of the war. It was a summer scene – even pleasant in its way.

Pleasant despite the fact that the soldiers wore field-grey instead of khaki. Pleasant despite the fact that they were enemies. Pleasant – no matter how Louis-Hercule, pacing at his side, glowering, might growl under his breath.

All down the *Quai de Paris* soldiers leaned against timeless stone and watched the sun strike the dancing water. Tugs fussed over barges above the *Ile Lacroix*. Swans stretched their necks out for bread. German regimental police, steel-helmeted despite the heat and with heavy crescent-shaped silver plates hanging from chains around their necks, moved carefully in step, eyes flashing this way and that, and saw only their own uniformed countrymen as their natural and implacable foes.

Along the *Quai* the trees rustled their leaves in a small wind off the river. Shadows as soft and as delicately drawn as the finest lace moved over male and female shoulders close together as couples leaned and looked out over the sun-drenched water – French women, German men.

At Quintain's side, Louis-Hercule's expression tightened. One of the girls with the German soldiers turned her head, and froze at the sight of the bitter and baleful expression in the old man's eyes.

As he hawked and spat his disgust she looked as though she had been struck across the face.

"We will remember . . ." he promised her, muttering. "There'll be some shaven heads in Rouen when the day of liberation dawns, my pretty one. And yours will be one of them!"

"Be quiet, mon vieux!" Quintain said sharply, and drew Louis-Hercule and Paul and Marianne after him, on and away down the *Quai*.

Rouen was an easy town to move around in. It was an easy town to feel free and at ease in – despite the presence of large numbers of enemy troops. They hadn't been bothered by the Germans, nor by the grey-garbed French Milice. Nor would they be, if only Louis-Hercule would keep a rein on his tongue and moved unhurriedly like everyone else.

Rouen was a leave town, and the civilian population was never subjected to irksome military control in leave towns – German or British. Rather the reverse was the case. Military officialdom was ready, willing and able to step in at any moment to protect the civilian population from the rude, licentious soldiery.

But all the same there were obvious limits to what could be done or said safely, without inviting some kind of official reaction. Louis-Hercule would have to be careful, Quintain thought. He'd have to keep his remarks to himself.

At all costs they mustn't draw any kind of official reaction or attention down upon themselves. At best, it would be

79

most unwelcome. More, it could be an utter disaster.

Quintain thought that he must never let his companions forget that there were possibly nearly as many Germans as Frenchmen at large in Rouen. He must never let them forget the blue-grey Renault van, now garaged on the outskirts of the city, nor the load that it carried. He must never let them forget what that load was intended for.

A special operation. An operation which must be carried through to its successful conclusion. Men's lives depended upon it. The lives of brave men.

"How much further to this cafe?" he asked Marianne when they had put a safe distance between themselves and the glowering, furious-eyed German soldier boy-friend of the French girl Louis-Hercule had growled at.

"How much further?"

"It's not far now," she told him, and there was an odd note in her voice, so that he looked at her quickly. Then, as if divining the chief question which lay uppermost in his mind, she added: "And they'll have waited."

"*Two hours*" Quintain had told the messenger who had brought news of the arrest of the leader of the Rouen Maquis. "*Two hours – to be on the safe side. And I'll meet all your people.*"

"*The Cafe des Deux Magots.*"

"*There in two hours –*" Quintain had told the messenger, shouting the words after him as he'd bumped out of the farmyard on Paul's *petrolette*.

That was what he'd said. But how many hours ago had that been? Six – or seven!

Of course, Quintain thought, it was the ambush on the road into Rouen which had made them late. The ambush, and all the other things which had stemmed out of it.

They could count themselves very lucky that they had survived the ambush. They hadn't been meant to survive it. None of them had been meant to survive it – with the exception of a certain traitor.

80

It had been a damned close call, Quintain thought. Too damned close by far. Sometime in the very near future he'd have to thank the traitor personally for that!

For it had been no accident that the Germans had been waiting in the roadside grove of poplars. No mere freak of chance which had made them swoop on the old Renault van rather than on any other van or truck. No accident at all – somehow the traitor in the Gournay en Bray Maquis had got word to them. Quintain was certain of that.

The only accidental thing about the ambush from the German point of view, was that it had misfired. That must be the traitor's point of view as well. The wrong people had been killed.

It had, of course, taken time to bury them.

And there had been Alphonse to bury, too. And one of the tyres of the van had had to be changed. And, after all that, when they'd finally got the Renault moving again, it had been to discover that more than one of its tyres had suffered in the short, sharp, savage affray with the Germans. Some bullets had found the engine.

They had limped into the outskirts of Rouen at snail's pace.

And there the Renault had had to be left in a garage owned by one of Rene's friends – for repair. Both Rene and Guillaume had elected to stay with it to keep an eye on its load. For the others, there had followed a long walk into the centre of the city.

Small wonder then that Quintain now asked himself if the men of the Rouen maquis would have waited for them. They had had six or seven hours to wait instead of the promised two, and they were bound to be jittery on this day, of all days, when their leader had been arrested by the Germans.

Would they have waited?

Quintain did not know. He had no means of knowing.

But one thing was certain. He had to go to the *Cafe des*

Deux Magots, and it wasn't far now. He had to go there to find out.

Then they reached the cafe. There were lace curtains at the windows, and it wasn't possible to see inside from the street, but the place seemed crowded.

Richard Quintain pushed open the door . . .

*

The door swung inwards, and sound came out. It beat around their heads as they hesitated on the threshold.

And they had good reason to hesitate. In a voice thick with suspicion, Louis-Hercule growled at Marianne: "Where have you brought us?"

It was a good question.

The sound which beat around them was a hubbub of voices. German voices. Nearly half the tables in the cafe were occupied by German soldiers.

They hadn't been able to see into the cafe from the street. But now they could see – now with German soldiers looking their way and a dozen conversations dying abruptly. Now they could see into what kind of place it was . . . now, when it was almost too late to retreat.

"I had no idea it would be like this. It isn't usually at this time of day –" In a defensive undertone Marianne was seeking to justify her choice of such an awkward place for a rendezvous.

Louis-Hercule and young Paul looked at her.

But – should they go in or not? Quintain had to make up his mind quickly. With every passing second their obvious indecision was attracting more and more attention.

They should hesitate no longer. They should go in now.

"Near the far wall . . . at the back." Louis-Hercule muttered without moving his lips, and then Quintain noticed a particular Frenchman. The Frenchman was looking their

82

way; a thin man with restless hands which betrayed his unease in this place.

Louis-Hercule and Quintain sat down next to the thin, young French civilian. They exchanged glances, but didn't speak. The two German soldiers at the next table eyed Marianne and then, after a quick, all-embracing scrutiny of her companions, which was met with a stony glare from Louis-Hercule, they looked away and continued talking together in low tones.

A waiter limped up, thin and old, and quietly asked Quintain for his order; behind the waiter bulged the broad back of a German N.C.O., noisily drinking *marc* at the next table. A stocky German senior N.C.O., with the red neck coming out over his uniform collar. He turned in his chair to paw the air in greeting and to leer in Marianne's direction, and then turned back to say something to the sycophantic group of garrison corporals at his table, which set them tittering.

Marianne was the only woman in the room, and the stocky German N.C.O.'s watery, drunken eye was upon her. His good eye. His only eye. The other was made of glass.

He had been talking loudly. Now he included Marianne in his audience, shifting in his seat.

"Barbarian!" Louis-Hercule muttered, and seized his drink as it arrived. He drained it in one gulp and set down the empty glass. "Let's get out of here!"

The thin, French civilian by his side made the first move. He pushed back his chair, got up, and went to pay the bill. But for the rest of them it wasn't going to be that easy.

The drunken N.C.O. was now firmly launched on a tale of his experiences on the Eastern front. A story of the previous summer, when the German armies had thrust into the Ukraine and swept all before them; when they'd crossed the Dneiper and taken Kharkov and Kiev.

"That's where it was —"

Loose-mouthed, wet-lipped, the German N.C.O. belched noisily.

He grinned drunkenly.

"– that's where it happened –"

"*Where what happened? Tell us!*"

Quintain and Marianne got up to go. Louis-Hercule and Paul were moving. But the N.C.O. slewed round in his chair to block the path of Quintain and Marianne to the door. They couldn't pass him.

"Seen you somewhere before –" he said, drunkenly waggish, to Marianne. "Seen you somewhere before, mam'-selle –"

"Do you mind!"

She attempted to push past him, and he made to thrust an arm around her waist. She twisted away from him, but stopped Quintain as he jerked forward angrily. "No – don't!"

"That's right. We don't want any trouble. You and I understand each other, eh?" The single bloodshot eye closed in a suggestive wink. "Especially now I remember where it was I saw you before –"

He stopped. His companions were becoming restive and impatient. "*Go on with the story! Tell us what happened . . .*"

Not moving his watery gaze from Marianne's face, the German said: "It was at Kiev. That's where it was. We were in the outskirts, fighting from street to street. Sometimes we had to take the same street twice or three times. Those mad dogs of Russians never seemed to know when they'd had enough. It was crazy really. We'd clear a street, killing or burning every Russian in it. They didn't have a chance. But somehow, during the night, more of 'em would creep back. More to be killed – more to be slaughtered . . ."

He laughed, screwing up his heavy, sweating face. His right eye, his glass eye, staring out of it expressionless and unmoving.

He went on: "But one morning we had 'em beaten, or so we thought. Beaten for good. They'd been blowing up stores all through the night. Fires were burning. The main Russian force had withdrawn and our Stukas were plastering hell out of it along the roads to the East. I was told to take my platoon and advance – advance through the outskirts to the centre of the city, winkling out any small, isolated pockets of resistance we might find along the way."

The German paused to wipe some of the sweat off his face with the back of his hand. He said: "It was like walking through a city of the dead. Nothing moving. No sound. Nothing alive. No birds even – until we were half-way across that square –"

"What square This is the first time you've mentioned it!"

"Be quiet!" the German N.C.O. growled. "Who's telling this story?"

He continued: "It was just an ordinary square. Ordinary by our standards then. A flat, open cement plain surrounded on four sides by heaps of smoking rubble. We weren't taking any chances, despite the fact that we'd struck no opposition until then. We were using all the cover we could. But still four of my men caught it out in the open. There was a machine-gun covering the square. Just one machine-gun in a heap of rubble that was more like dust than bricks and mortar. Just one machine-gun, only one – and yet it caused us more trouble than a regiment of Ivans would have done."

He laughed again. A phlegmy sound. He threw back his head and drained his glass of *marc*. And still his right eye, his glass eye, glittered.

He said: "We could have by-passed the square, of course, but that wasn't in my orders. And I didn't feel much like by-passing it, either, not with four of my best men dead. So, to cut a long story short, we had quite a battle with the machine-gunner and we won it. We coaxed her out with flame-throwers in the end. Yes, it was a woman. And we got her alive."

"And what happened? What did you do to her?"

One of the corporals around the table grinned. "What do you think?"

"They brought her to me," the stocky German senior N.C.O. continued, "and she was a beauty, I'll tell you! She was something special – nothing like the ordinary peasant woman. But my men brought her to me and some of them wanted to kill her because she'd killed four of their comrades and some of the others were prepared to forget their comrades –"

The German's lips were plump and wet.

"– You know how it is –"

"*But what happened?*"

"I felt sorry for her," the German N.C.O. grinned, and moved hands which shone like the white, soft under-bellies of long-dead fish. "I didn't want to see her killed. When the heat of the fighting's over I've got a soft spot for women – beautiful women . . ."

His eyes – the good one bloodshot, the false on, the right one, brittle and staring – moved to rest on Marianne; moved sideways to touch Quintain. His voice was thick with a double-meaning; an innuendo Quintain couldn't fully understand.

"I don't like to see them hurt – unnecessarily –"

"So what did you do?"

The stocky German N.C.O. switched his gaze, a trifle unwillingly back to his companions. "I made things easy for her," he said. "I told her she wouldn't be killed – nor would my men have their way with her – if only she'd answer me one question. A simple question. One question, and I'd protect her –"

Someone round the table laughed wetly until he began to hiccup. "I don't know how you phrased the question, but I know the answer you wanted. It was 'yes', wasn't it? What's that in Russian?"

"I'm not as crude as you are," the stocky German said. He said it smiling. "Not nearly as crude as you are –"

"Then what was your question?"

"I told her I'd be her protector if she'd answer me –" the

sweating German senior N.C.O. leaned forward "– if she'd answer me which of my eyes was made of glass."

"That is a simple one! The right one. It's easy."

"Yes –" said the N.C.O., and leaned back. There was a short silence.

"But what did she say?" someone asked. "The story doesn't finish there! What happened?"

The German N.C.O. turned his head. He was looking at Marianne again. Looking at her lingeringly. "In the same situation, what would *you* have said, mam'selle? What would *you* have said if you'd been that Russian woman?"

Again his voice was thick. Again there was a double-meaning in his words.

Marianne hesitated, but not for long. Then she said clearly: "I'd have said what the Russian woman did –"

"You've heard the story before?" one of the corporals around the table asked her.

"No, but it can only have one ending –"

The cafe was very quiet.

"I'd have said what the Russian woman said. The left eye must be the glass eye –"

"The left eye? But it's obvious –"

"The left eye," Marianne said firmly.

"Why? the stocky German senior N.C.O. demanded angrily. "Why?"

"Because," Marianne said calmly, "the right one is the only one with any humanity and intelligence in it!"

There was a roar of laughter from the German soldiers in the cafe. A roar of laughter in which the corporals around the table did not dare to join. The senior N.C.O. did not join in it either. He said, his face twisted with fury: "You'll regret that, mam'selle!"

She pushed past him.

"You'll regret that!"

Quintain made to go on, pushing Marianne ahead of him, but a hand fell upon his arm. A hard hand. He had to stop

87

"You!" the thickset German N.C.O. growled. "I want a word with you!"

And, as a sudden silence fell over the cafe, and all eyes were sharp-focused on Quintain and on the German behind him, the Englishman was forced around.

*

Elsewhere in northern France that afternoon, there was a man called Maddox.

Maddox was an Englishman, and he was young, barely thirty. But no-one thought it to look at him. He had the white hair and lined face of an old man.

Maddox, was a naval officer, a British naval officer, and he had had three ships go down beneath him on the Arctic convoys to Murmansk.

Of the last one – of a complement of eight hundred and seventy-two men, he was the sole survivor.

The first time he had had a ship sunk beneath him, he had been in the water for only six minutes before being picked up. Six short minutes which had seemed like an eternity, as he had fought the icy fingers of freezing death.

In Arctic seas, it is not easy for a man to stay alive – even for six minutes. He has to consciously war with the elements for his life throughout every second.

He is plunged in water which is anything up to a hundred degrees below his body temperature. He must move and keep on moving as the strength pours out of him like a torrent. Somehow he must try to stop his blood turning to ice.

Six short minutes can be a very, very long time in an Arctic sea. But the second time Maddox had a ship torpedoed beneath him, he was in the water even longer. Much longer. That time he had to fight to stay alive for nearly an hour.

But the third time, the last time, was the worst of all. It was the time beside which every other terrible experience Maddox had ever had paled into insignificance. It was the time when, at the last minute, a boat was launched from the doomed ship, and Maddox counted himself lucky to be able to claw his way aboard. That time he had been in the water for only the few seconds it had taken him to reach the lifeboat. Just those few frantic seconds. But it was a time of ghastly, unendurable horror none-the-less.

The convoy which Maddox's ship had been defending was under heavy U-boat attack. A night attack. Maddox's ship was sunk a few minutes after midnight and during what remained of the hours of darkness there had been no opportunity for any of the other escort vessels, hardpressed as they were, to leave the convoy and search for survivors.

In consequence the lifeboat had fallen behind the convoy during the night, and when the thin, cruelly cold Arctic dawn had come, the boat had been alone – completely alone – on an empty, endless, storm-wracked, slate-coloured sea.

Eighteen days Maddox had sailed in that boat. Eighteen days, during which time every one of his companions had perished – very slowly. Eighteen days, towards the end of which, mercifully, Maddox went out of his mind.

When the lifeboat, by chance, was blown on to a beach in the Shetlands, it had taken four strong fishermen to hold down the raving, screeching husk of a man Maddox had become. A man who fought them over the putrefied corpses of eight companions . . .

After that incident, and after four months in hospital, Their Lordships of the Admiralty had thought that Maddox merited a change of scene and a change of job. Perhaps he even merited a rest. So he was seconded to Naval Intelligence for these reasons – and for one other. He spoke three European languages fluently.

And that is how he enters this story, and why. For as Richard Quintain entered the *Cafe des Deux Magots* in Rouen late in the afternoon of Monday, the seventeenth of August, nineteen forty-two, Maddox was leaving Dieppe.

He was leaving the town after spending two days there under the very noses of the Germans. He was leaving to return to Portsmouth by submarine later that night.

He had been sent to Dieppe by Naval Intelligence to secure first-hand, up-to-the-minute information on the state of the German defences – much the same kind of job that Quintain himself had earlier undertaken at St. Nazaire.

Maddox had been landed on a beach fifteen kilometres west of the town, midway between Dieppe and St. Valery-en-Caux, and from the same beach he would be taken off again.

He would take with him a lot of vital information. He had talked to Frenchmen and Frenchwomen living in and around Dieppe and he had done his job well.

One point had been brought out in conversations again and again, and it was lodged tight in his mind. He would repeat it, with emphasis, to his superiors when he got back to England.

The E-boat base to the east of Dieppe must be accounted for before the landing began. Everything he had learned convinced him that this was absolutely and vitally necessary.

At best, the operation planned against Dieppe was very risky. But, and he would say this with all the vehemence at his command, unless the E-boat base were completely neutralized, together with all the craft in it, Operation Jubilee would be more than risky – very much more.

It would be an unqualified and unprecedented disaster.

CHAPTER TEN

"YOU! I want a word with you!" the thick-set German voice growled behind Quintain. A hard hand fastened upon his arm, forcing him around.

"You –" he said, and scraped back his chair, and he swayed on his feet. "You – fraulein –"

And he was neither looking at Quintain nor actually talking to him. It was doubtful if he was even aware of the existence of the Englishman, despite the fact that he had fastened a hand on Quintain's arm and jerked him around.

He had eyes only for Marianne. It was she he was really addressing. "You – come here!" His hands flapped and he nearly fell over. "Come here and tell me why – why . . ." He hiccupped loudly.

Marianne, after an initial momentary hesitation, went on past him. The German N.C.O. tried to grab her arm as she passed him ."You hear what I say? Come here –!"

His chair went over with a crash.

"Come here, you –"

And then it happened.

Sound rushed back to fill the cafe, and simultaneously growling in his throat, Louis-Hercule thrust forward massively to reach the N.C.O. But he never did.

The old bull found himself being pushed out of the way. Quintain was pushed out of the way, too.

A voice said curtly: "This is our affair!"

Two military policemen had appeared out of nowhere to flank the N.C.O. An officer struck him a vicious back-handed blow across the face.

"*Schwein!* Remember your manners! Remember where you are, and who you are! *Dumkopf!*"

The stocky N.C.O. sat down hurriedly. He sat down on a

91

chair which wasn't there any more. He was dragged up from the floor and bundled out of the cafe with very scant ceremony.

Then the officer returned.

Marching up to Quintain and Marianne, Louis-Hercule and Paul, he snapped his heels together and bowed curtly and stiffly. "My apologies, mam'selle – messieurs –"

Another bow. A salute. "Heil Hitler!" And he was gone, and Quintain let the pent-up breath come out of him slowly.

Then, as the thin French civilian who had been sitting at the back of the cafe pushed past him on his way to the door –

"Let's get out of here!" Quintain said.

He followed the thin man out – to stop abruptly. The Frenchman had not gone far, nor got far. A Citroen *traction avant* – the front-wheel drive French saloon favoured by the Security Police – was at the edge of the pavement. Two grim-eyed men had their hands on the French civilian.

"*La Geste!*" hissed Louis-Hercule. "Gestapo!"

A third man crossed the pavement quickly. He reached them.

"Your papers." He made the demand flatly and unemotionally. His voice was like his eyes – empty. "Your papers."

They produced them, one by one, Quintain last. It was the first time he'd ever had to produce his papers. They were very clever forgeries, of course. They were the best. They were Made in England and, as forgeries went, they were quite superb.

But would they fool the Gestapo?

*

The Gestapo agent was tall and broad and heavily built.

He was middle-aged and the years had run to his middle. His fingers were a little clumsy as they unfolded the identification documents one by one.

92

He took his time.

In an ominous silence he inspected the documents very carefully, then he looked up abruptly.

There was an unfathomable expression in his close-set eyes as he stared at each one of the four of them in turn. Then he spoke, and his voice was deep and harsh.

"You –"

He threw the word at the young Paul. "You! – come over here! Come with me!"

He moved off a little way and snapped angrily at Paul when he turned to find that the tall, blond Alsatian was hesitating, and that he hadn't even begun to follow him. "Come here! How many times do I have to tell you? Come here!"

And Paul went.

He stood on the edge of the pavement with the Gestapo agent, and the two of them talked, Paul shifting his feet very uncomfortably. Not one word of what passed between them was audible to Louis-Hercule, to Marianne, or to Quintain.

"What's going on?" From beneath thick, bushy brows the old bull of Gournay-en-Bray glowered in the direction of Paul and the Gestapo agent. "What are they talking about, I wonder?"

He turned his head to shoot a quick glance at the other Gestapo men beside the *traction avant*. The thin Frenchman from the cafe was handcuffed now, and he returned Louis-Hercule's glance bitter-eyed.

Louis-Hercule moved uneasily.

Under his breath he muttered to Quintain: "I don't like the look of this at all! Should we run for it?"

Quintain's lips barely moved. "How far would we get?" It was a good question.

The Gestapo men by the car looked as solid and aggressively capable as the third man talking to Paul. If they ran they wouldn't get far – that was sure!

"I still don't like the look of it," Louis-Hercule persisted.

"He's still got our papers. And what's Paul telling him –?"

The tall, blond young man was certainly telling him something. He was talking vehemently, his hands moving.

"What's he saying?" Louis-Hercule muttered suspiciously.

But they couldn't hear what was being said, and all further conjecture was cut short by the middle-aged Gestapo agent swinging round. He left Paul standing and came back across the pavement heavy-footed and pugnacious; jut-jawed.

Paul came after him, but moved hesitantly. He didn't look at Quintain. It seemed he was being very careful not to look at him. The Gestapo agent did.

"You! – you're coming with us!"

"But –"

"No arguments!" The close-set eyes were narrowed. The heavy head jerked. "In the car! Get in the car! I'm taking you to Headquarters."

"Are you arresting me?"

The Gestapo man snarled: "I told you to get in the car! Now get a move on!"

Quintain shot a quick glance around him. A number of German soldiers had spilled out of the doorway of the *Cafe des Deux Magots* and now stood, watching warily. One of the Gestapo men with the handcuffed prisoner had produced a Mauser pistol.

Quintain made himself relax. Marianne looked strained and tense and white, but Quintain even managed to smile.

"In the car! Move!" The big Gestapo agent repeated impatiently.

Louis-Hercule touched Quintain, laid a hand on his shoulder. The Gestapo man struck it away. "Move!"

And Quintain had no choice but to obey. He climbed into the car and the door slammed behind him.

CHAPTER ELEVEN

RICHARD QUINTAIN stood in a big, broad room in Gestapo Headquarters in Rouen. The floor was mirror-polished. This was the first thing that Quintain noticed; the fact that you could, quite literally, see your face in the floor. The second thing he noticed was the bowl of flowers.

They were blood-red flowers in a bowl on a broad desk near shuttered windows. Their scent was heavy on the still air.

Light fell through the shutters and slatted the polished floor. Golden light. The light of early evening. Quintain was alone in the room. This was where the Gestapo men had brought him, and left him. There was no-one behind the desk near the shuttered windows.

Quintain moved restlessly and then stopped. He turned. Someone was entering the room. The door behind him was opening. He thought then of all he had ever heard or read about the Gestapo. He knew that he must have been brought here to answer questions. He waited to see who would come through the doorway and he expected to see a man twice as big and four times as ugly as the one who had brought him here.

He expected to see another middle-aged man, heavy-jowled like the first. And mean-eyed, like the first, but this one with an even more limited supply of patience. His inquisitor.

It would go well with the flowers on the desk. And blood would neither penetrate nor stain the mirror-polished boards of the floor.

This was Gestapo Headquarters. He knew what to expect. And then, through the doorway, instead of an ugly, heavy-jowled, middle-aged man, there came a woman. And she was beautiful.

*

She was beautiful, and blonde, and tall, and slim. Her eyes were very blue. She came into the room, paused to close the door behind her, and then regarded Quintain very speculatively for a long moment.

Then she moved away from the door and passed in front of him. She went to the desk beside the shuttered windows, and smoothed the skirt of her carefully tailored black business suit as she sat. She moved a long-fingered hand, and Quintain sat too. In silence. And it was a silence which lengthened as the blonde studied him frankly and interestedly over her desk.

Then she spoke – suddenly. "You know why you're here?"

The young woman spoke in French and Quintain answered her in the same language. "No."

"You know who I am?"

"No."

"My name is Anna Heyster. That means nothing to you?"

"No."

One of the young woman's eyebrows edged up a little. Then, with a tight smile, she said: "You haven't been long in Rouen?"

"No."

"How long?" she shot at him swiftly; and now she spoke in English.

Quintain frowned and looked helpless. He shrugged as if he didn't understand what she was saying.

"How long?" she repeated, this time in French, and showed her small white teeth in another tight smile.

"How long? Only a few hours," Quintain said.

"You came from where?"

"From Gournay-en-Bray."

"Why?"

"I had business here."

"What business?"

The questions were coming thick and fast.

"I work on a farm. There was produce to sell."

"What produce?"

A cover story had been arranged.

"Eggs and —"

"How did you come?"

"In a car —"

"Those others came with you? The ones who were with you when you were detained?"

"Yes."

"Which way did you come from Gournay-en-Bray?"

There was a cover story for this, too. Quintain had memorized a route which avoided the grove of poplars, the ambush, and the German dead.

She didn't wait for him to finish, but interrupted flatly: "You are not French?"

"No," Quintain admitted.

"What are you?"

"Basque. Before the war I —"

She interrupted again. "What is your name?"

She had his identity papers on the desk in front of her. Quintain could see them. But, when he didn't answer within a split second, she repeated her demand impatiently. "Your name, man! Your name!"

"Tomas Cuervo."

She was writing it down. Without looking up, she frowned, paused, and said in a perfectly ordinary voice, and in English: "How do you spell it?"

Quintain's mouth almost opened but he caught himself just in time. He looked blank. He said nothing. And Anna Heyster lifted her head and stared at him.

Then abruptly she said: "Stand up!" And she had reverted to French again.

Quintain hesitated.

She had thumbed a button on her desk. "Stand up!" The door of the room came open behind him.

He stood up.

"Now turn around . . ."

She spoke lingeringly, as if with quiet enjoyment. He obeyed her.

Three men blocked the doorway. Three men in the dread black uniform of the Gestapo. There were heavy revolvers at their hips and their hands were not far from them.

Behind Quintain, Anna Heyster was moving. She came up behind him and something hard and cold dug into the back of his neck. The tiny hairs stood on end along his spine. He moved –

"Stand still!"

He heard the unmistakeable snick of a revolver being cocked and knew what the cold and hard thing was that bored into him.

Anna Heyster said very quietly, and in English: "I know who you really are, and what you are. You have been betrayed."

Quintain's heart thudded, but not one of his muscles moved. He had to fight hard to keep the right expression on his face. He was Tomas Cuervo, a Basque. He didn't understand English.

But Anna Heyster still spoke in this language.

"You are a British agent, and I am Anna Heyster, the chief of the *Geheimestaatspolizei* in Rouen. I am surprised that you have not heard of me. I have been the death of many of your countrymen. I will be your death, too."

And her voice carried conviction. It was quiet, but all the more deadly for that.

"I am going to count three. You have just three seconds to tell me why you have been sent here. Just three seconds to live, if you don't."

Still she spoke in English, the language Quintain had feigned not to understand.

"I know you understand me," she said. "I know who you really are. I know you have understood every word I have said. I am going to count three. I am starting now. No-one can save you. *One* –"

The Gestapo men in the doorway had eased out their revolvers. Whatever Quintain did, there was no escape.

"No-one can help you if you do not tell me the truth. *Two* –"

Quintain's mouth was dry. His throat was dry.

"You have one more second. Just one more second."

"What are you saying," Quintain asked querulously in French. "What is happening?"

Anna Heyster laughed at him, a short sound.

The last second was a lifetime. He felt the blonde's grip tighten on her gun as she took second pressure on the trigger.

"*Three*," she said.

And she fired.

*

She fired the gun.

The hammer fell.

But only on an empty chamber.

Quintain was cold with sweat, but he still fought to wear the right expression and say the right things. He still fought to be Tomas Cuervo – which was the name on the identity documents he'd been given before he'd left England.

So he stood there, and the questions fell out of him until she cut through them curtly, still speaking in English: "You are a brave man. I could have killed you. I might have killed you. I might still . . ."

Then her voice softened subtly. "But I like brave men. I respect them. You can turn around again now, and sit down."

But she was still speaking English, and Quintain stayed where he was.

She seemed to lose patience with him then. "Turn around!" she snapped, still in English.

99

"What are you saying to me? I don't understand?"

"Turn around, damn you!" She swore at him in French, and in French she gave the order. Then Quintain obeyed her and heard the door close behind him. Had the three Gestapo men gone?

The blonde's expression was an angry one, for a moment. Then suddenly she relaxed, shrugged, and smiled. "Have a cigarette."

She pushed an enamel sil/er box across the desk towards him, and a small two-pin plug fell off the desk on to the floor and rolled a few feet.

Quintain retrieved the plug and replaced it on the desk. "Thank you," said Anna Heyster. "We'll speak in French, if that's what you prefer."

The cigarettes in the enamelled box were English. An exclusive and expensive brand of Super Virginia.

"You always smoke these, I think," Anna Heyster said. "This is your brand – when you can get them. You see –" her shoulders moved and her red lips pouted as she smiled. "– I really do know quite a lot about you."

"You are mistaken," Quintain said stubbornly. "My name is Tomas Cuer –"

"But take one just the same," she said, interrupting him, and pushed the box nearer. Shrugging, he accepted, and she took a cigarette also.

Then she looked around the desk for a lighter; couldn't see one. Quintain produced one almost automatically. Her eyes on his, she steadied his hand as he lit her cigarette for her, and took the lighter from him.

It was an expensive-looking lighter, and its clean, uncluttered lines looked very English. But it was, in fact. Made in Germany . . .

She gave him the lighter back, and blew smoke. "A careful man as well as a brave one," she said.

"I don't know what you're talking about . . ."

She relaxed in her chair and crossed her long slim legs.

She relaxed completely, like a cat. She regarded him appraisingly from beneath half-lowered lids. Then she said: "You are on the wrong side, you know. We Germans know how to look after brave men. They get the best. The best of everything. You should think about that."

Quintain said: "I still don't quite understand what you're talking about. I –"

"There's no need to pretend. We are quite alone here," she told him. "There are no hidden microphones. We are completely alone . . ."

Her voice lingered over the words and then, suddenly, she moved. Colour came back into her cheeks. She stubbed out her cigarette viciously, and twisted around in her chair. She turned her face from him. She said, angrily: "I could be stupid about you. There was another man once – another brave man. Another Englishman. He brought me a lot of trouble."

She was standing now, her back towards him. Her blonde hair just touched her shoulders. She was looking through the slatted shutters into the dying light of the day. "Brave men are my weakness," she said.

Then she turned and looked at him again, saying nothing now, just looking, and it seemed to Quintain that she had spoken the truth.

She said quickly, almost breathlessly: "You can trust me. I can help you . . ."

And, after that, there was another silence, a long silence, a silence broken only by the quick sound of her breathing as she stood there, close to him, her eyes intent on his face.

Then Quintain said: "My name is Tomas Cuervo. I am a Basque. I do not know who you have mistaken me for but –"

The spell was broken.

Anna Heyster jerked away from him.

Taut-faced, she went behind her desk. She sat down. She thumbed the bell-push and once more the door opened behind Quintain. He heard it open. The beautiful blonde wasn't looking at him now. Her face was averted.

"Take him away," she said curtly.

Hard footsteps sounded behind Quintain. He twisted round. There were Gestapo men behind him. Gestapo men with heavy revolvers. He got out: "I have done nothing wrong. I came to Rouen to sell eggs and –"

Abruptly she raised a hand, stopping him. The men advancing on him stopped too.

Then: "Your papers," she said, and pushed them towards him.

He picked them up.

She looked at the men behind him. "Take him back to the place where you found him," she said, and she spoke in German. "And leave him there."

Quintain said, as a man mystified. "I am free to go?"

"You will be taken back to the *Cafe des Deux Magots*," she said. Her mouth twisted. "You disappoint me. You seem to be all that you claim to be . . ."

Quintain muttered: "I don't understand –"

Then he made his voice sound indignant. "But why was I brought here at all? I have done no wrong. I –"

"I told you," she answered. "Information was laid against you. What else could we do but bring you in for questioning?"

But even this reasonable-sounding answer was a trap.

For she had not spoken in French. He shook his head as if baffled by what she was saying.

She stood up. She said: "Take him away."

The Gestapo men stood back. Anna Heyster gestured and Quintain got up, and was ushered towards the door. Just as he reached it, Anna Heyster said quickly: "Wait a minute. Wait!"

But Quintain didn't even check his pace. Not even voluntarily. Anna Heyster had spoken English again, and Tomas Cuervo didn't understand English.

He had one last glimpse of her standing by her desk. one hand resting near the bowl of blood-red flowers, looking coldly beautiful.*

Then he was out of the room and walking down a long and cold corridor with Gestapo men on either side of him. The corridor led to the street.

*Anne Heyster did not survive the war. Towards the end of 1942 she was transferred from Gestapo Headquarters in Rouen to the region of Saone et Louire, and she was there, at Macon, when the Allies and the Maquis together made a determined effort to expel the Germans from France in August 1944.

Caught up in the fighting, Anna Heyster tried to escape to Germany, but was captured by the Maquis near Poligny. Her lover of the moment, a Gestapo officer named Staarden, was taken with her. Both, at a summary Court Martial, were sentenced by the Maquis – into whose hands they had fallen – to be shot. Before being killed, Anne was gang-raped repeatedly, and forced to dig her own grave.

The exact whereabouts of her burial place is unknown.

CHAPTER TWELVE

UNDER the empty glare of unshaded electric lights, half a dozen old and painfully tired vehicles dotted the concrete floor of the cavernous garage.

The blue-grey Renault van stood near a rear wall, and there was no-one working on it. Quintain swore under his breath.

Tools were there. An inspection lamp hung over the Renault's gutted engine, burning brightly. But no-one was actually working on the van.

By Quintain's side, the short, swarthy Rene grunted. "They're all up there." He jerked his head towards the grimy window of an office which looked out over the garage floor. "They thought you were done for. Finished."

Quintain said angrily. "They didn't check very thoroughly, did they? They didn't check at all – nor leave anyone waiting at the cafe. And why has all work stopped on repairing the van?"

"They're arguing it out," Rene said. "It was young Paul's idea."

Quintain shot a swift glance at the cracked face of an old clock on the wall. It was ten in the evening. The van was still unserviceable and zero hour – his personal zero hour – was now little more than twenty-four hours away. Time was running out. His mouth set.

He made for the steel stairway which climbed to the office. He had one foot on the first tread when Rene stopped him. "I'm sentry. I've got to get back outside. But before I go, there's something I've got to get off my chest –"

There he hesitated.

Quintain eyed him. "Go on."

Rene's eyes were empty as the words came. "There's a

traitor in this Maquis, isn't there? Someone working hand-in-glove with the Germans. Someone who betrayed Gerard and all the other men who were killed or taken at the same time. Someone who's still trading in treachery."

The way Rene spoke the words made them into a series of statements, not questions.

Quintain said: "Are you just guessing, or –"

"I've known for a long time," Rene said slowly. "I've never had any proof, but I've known. Things have been bad for this maquis ever since –"

He hesitated again.

"Since what," said Quintain.

"Since . . . well, since *he* came."

"Who."

But Rene wouldn't answer. He shook his head. "I'll say nothing more. I could be wrong."

It was maddening. Quintain said sharply: "You have got to tell me what you know!"

"I could be wrong," Rene insisted stubbornly. "But add things up for yourself. See if you get the same answer that I did. And –" He patted the automatic which bulged out of the leather *canadian* jacket he wore. "– you can rely on me, and on this, absolutely. If you want me, if you need me, just shout . . ."

*

Paul's guttural and impassioned voice reached Quintain as he stood at the head of the steel stairway.

It reached him as he thrust out a hand to open the door of the office, and it made him hesitate.

"This 'special operation' is off!" Paul was saying emphatically. "Of course it's off! It must be off! We don't even know the target, so how can we go through with it?"

"Marianne must know the target." Louis-Hercule's voice also reached Quintain. And it was stubborn. "You do know, don't you, Marianne? But you're not telling!"

"I know no more than you do," Marianne retorted. "He never confided in me."

"I don't believe you!" Louis-Hercule made the statement in an angry, snarling growl. "You're working hand-in-glove with Paul! You're up to something, the pair of you. You want to stop this special operation dead in its tracks, that's why you won't tell us the target."

"That's not true!"

"But it is true that you and Paul are up to something. Why else have you been whispering together all day? What were you talking about in the truck on the way here – and before that. And where were you just before we set out from the farm, Paul?"

"He went into the wood. That's where he keeps his pigeons." It was Guillaume speaking now, and speaking bitterly. "Carrier-pigeons, eh, Paul?"

"That's a lie!"

"How odd that I saw a pigeon take off from the wood just a few minutes before we started out from the farm – while you were still missing!"

"I don't know – or care – what you saw!"

"But the Germans knew which route we were taking, didn't they?"

"I don't know what they knew. I didn't tell them."

"But you were talking to that Gestapo agent outside the cafe for a long time," Louis-Hercule put in silkily. "What did you tell him?"

"Nothing of any consequence. I've already told you!" Paul sounded exasperated. "He saw from my papers that I came from Alsace. He didn't speak good French and, as an Alsatian, he knew that I would speak German. That's all there was to it. I've told you. That's why he picked on me to question."

"And you answered every one of his questions, but you are evading mine!" Louis-Hercule bellowed. "What did you tell him."

106

"Nothing. I told him nothing."

"Nothing –?" Louis-Hercule almost choked on the word. "Yet, immediately afterwards, the Englishman is arrested!"

"They didn't arrest him. You've no proof that they arrested him."

"The *Geste* took him!" Louis-Hercule snarled. "Don't split hairs with me! So they didn't arrest him – but they took him, didn't they. And we all know what happens to a man when the *Geste* get their filthy hands on him! I went down to the Kommandantur tonight, asking as many questions as I dared, and no-one knows anything. It's as if 'Tomas' had never existed! And then I come back here –" Louis-Hercule's voice had begun to climb to a bull-like bellow again "– I come back here, and what do I find? You, Paul have taken it upon yourself to give orders in my absence! You told them to stop work on the Renault!"

"Well –" Paul demanded "– what was the use of having men sweat and lose sleep to finish the job? We don't know what target the Englishman has in mind. So the 'special operation' is off. It must be! And, in any case, before we take that Renault out on the streets again it's going to have to be repainted a different colour, and the plates are going to have to be changed. If it really was us those Germans were waiting for in that poplar grove, the description of the van will have been circulated."

"What do you mean – 'if it really was us'?" Guillaume sneered. "You know, don't you? What doubt is there? Who would know better than you!"

"*Ta bouche!*" Paul snarled. "Shut up!" And then, as Guillaume angrily interrupted again, the young Alsatian raised his voice to shout him down. "I tell you, I'm not going out in that van again until it has been repainted!"

"Oh, but you are!" Louis-Hercule growled.

And, as he 'spoke, so he moved. And moved abruptly. Quintain heard him. And he also heard Paul say querulously: "What are you doing?" The question ended on a high note. "What are you doing with that –"

"It's a gun; it's loaded, and it's pointing at you!" Louis-Hercule spoke with savage satisfaction. "It might even go off! And if it did, I wouldn't be sorry."

"Nor I," said Guillaume.

"But I'm just showing it to you," Louis-Hercule continued. "Just showing it to you, and telling you that you're going to do as I say. I lead again in the Gournay-en-Bray maquis! When I tell you to do a thing, then you'll do it! I'll have no arguments! And what I'm telling you now – all of you – is that whatever had happened to 'Tomas' isn't going to stop this 'special operation' going forward."

Paul said, almost despairingly: "And I keep telling you –"

"That we don't know the target?" Louis-Hercule laughed shortly. "But Marianne knows. Even if she doesn't she can soon find out. The Englishman's transmitter is in the van, Marianne. Go and get it!"

"But –"

"You heard what I said! Go and get it! And then call London. Tell them what has happened and ask for the target. We are going to complete the job that 'Tomas' began. You hear that, Paul? I'm back in command again, and nothing has changed. We carry on as if the Englishman was still with us!"

And that was when Quintain moved, unable to resist the theatrical.

He pushed open the door.

"I *am* still with you," he said.

CHAPTER THIRTEEN

ALL through the night they had worked on the van. Then, late on the following morning, they had collected and loaded the high-explosive they had come to Rouen to obtain. And they had loaded it without incident, and set off once more.

It was now noon and, under a broiling sun, they were out on the road again. Out on the road with the van no longer blue-grey but green, and its number-plates changed. There had been sound sense in some of Paul's arguments, Quintain reflected.

The van rattled and swayed over the roads. It was travelling due north. Quintain was being very careful. Only he knew exactly where they were going. He was taking no chances. The others would not know until the very last possible moment.

"Swing left at the next fork," he told Felix, in the driver's seat. Left, right, or straight ahead, he gave the orders as and when they were necessary.

He didn't want any of the others to know where they were going – not yet. There was a traitor amongst them. He could never forget it.

And the traitor amongst them must not know where they were going until it was absolutely impossible for that knowledge to be shared with the Germans.

*

The same sun which blazed down on the now green Renault van, shone over transports using English roads, too.

Troop transports rumbled along the dusty roads in English counties, growled past the squat Saxon churches in the old villages, snorted and snuffled through narrow High

109

Streets past ancient inns, and headed South to reach the English Channel.

Troop-transport after troop-transport in what seemed like an endless procession struck through Hampshire and Sussex to reach four ports: Southampton, Portsmouth, Shoreham and Newhaven. And, in those four ports, the little ships – hundreds of them – were waiting.

The troop transports emptied on the outskirts of the four towns. Five thousand Canadian infantrymen jumped over tailboards into the road and formed up in columns. Then they marched through the town to the docks.

They marched through streets lined with strangely silent civilians. There was the crunch, crunch, crunch of steel-shod boots hitting the road perfectly in time, and there was nothing else. No-one cheered, no-one laughed, no-one sang. There were no bands.

Five thousand Canadians marched to the ships which were to take them to France, and in the heavy silence all around the sound of their marching feet and the occasional jangle of metal on metal was curiously ominous.

It sounded mechanical, and inhuman.

Men were to remark, even years later, that in some odd way, it sounded dead.

Once aboard the transports, the boats and the barges, the Canadians were at last told where they were going. Many received the news with consternation.

Dieppe –?

But – bloody hell – that was where they'd been bound for last time, until the raid had been called off.

They thought of all the talking they'd done afterwards in pubs all along the south coast, and they looked at each other furtively, and then looked away.

Good God! Dieppe!

A strange tension gripped the entire Canadian Division. A tension which went far beyond that which might be expected to fasten its icy fingers on men about to undergo their baptism of fire.

It was the tension born of every normally latent animal instinct: that tension which tells a man with dread certainty that he is about to see the face of Death.

The entire Candian Division received the news – Destination Dieppe – with the grimmest forebodings, and with good reason.

Of the five thousand Canadians who marched that day to the boats, fewer than two thousand were to return.

*

A man called Maddox made his personal report to the Chiefs of the Combined Operations' Planning Staff at Number Eleven Group Headquarters.

Maddox looked very tired.

The news of his return from France by submarine, and word of the contents of his report, spread rapidly through all the upper echelons of command and created furious maelstroms of activity.

The red telephone was busy on a desk in a vast office carved out of one of the galleries of the Natural History Museum in South Kensington.

"Is everything going to be all right, Fenner? Are you sure?"

"A hell of a lot depends upon your organization, Fenner! Can you be absolutely certain – *absolutely confident* – that those E-boat pens will be destroyed in time?"

Secretly, Felix Fenner was confident of nothing. What wise man was in this third year of war? But his reason told him that if the job could be done, then, somehow, Quintain would do it. *If* it could be done.

A message had been received by radio from Quintain that morning. A message which mentioned serious, unwelcome, and unexpected delays in carrying the special operation through to its successful conclusion. Some delays had to be allowed for. The possibility of unforeseen circumstances had been taken into account. But suppose there were more delays along the way? Felix Fenner didn't like to think about it, but he had to. Supposing the unexpected happened again, and again, and again? What about that?

Would Quintain still manage to complete his assignment in time? Would he be able to rendezvous with the men who were actually going to position and detonate the explosive in time for them to carry out this, the most vital part, of the whole plan?

Fenner's red telephone rang again and again throughout the long, drowsy August afternoon. "Are you certain about those E-boat pens, Fenner? Everything depends on them being blown sky-high at the right moment!"

Felix Fenner could only tell his callers what they wanted to hear; that everything was under control. That everything would be all right. But privately he paced the floor of his vast, baronial office, tugging his red beard, gnawing his lip, wondering . . .

There were now less than ten hours to go to zero. Would Quintain complete his mission successfully? Would the E-boat pens be accounted for before the first Canadians streaked in towards the Dieppe beaches?

A lot of men were going to die, screaming in the water under merciless E-boat machine-guns, if Quintain failed!

Cynic and sceptic though he was, Fenner found himself silently praying as darkness fell. A host of men had now been committed to the dawn assault on Dieppe whatever happened.

CHAPTER FOURTEEN

ALREADY, at fifteen minutes after noon on that Tuesday, the eighteenth of August, nineteen forty-two, the ninth and thirteenth mine-sweeping flotillas had set sail from Portsmouth to clear two channels through the German-laid minefields off the French coast.

From Portsmouth they had followed an inshore track towards Newhaven at first, so that if they were observed by enemy aircraft their true purpose in putting out to sea would not be anticipated.

At the same time, in Newhaven, Shoreham and Portsmouth, under the cover of man-made smoke, twenty-four tank-landing craft loaded Churchill tanks. Elsewhere, in the same ports, a total assault force of six thousand and eighty-six officers and men, Canadian infantry and British Commandos, was embarked on nine infantry landing ships and a host of smaller vessels. By the time that dusk came, all was ready. This part of the operation was complete.

And, shortly before dusk fell, the ninth and thirteenth mine-sweeping flotillas altered course for France, and dropped the first green-flagged Dan to mark what was to be the entrance to the most westerly of the two channels they were sweeping.

The time was ten minutes after six.

Not much after this, that part of the assault force based on Newhaven set sail for France and Dieppe.

Operation Jubilee was under way.

That night there was a high moon and a false half-light, and it was difficult for lookouts to do their job or to be certain of distances. The Dan they were trying to see carried a faint green light, but it was lost in the shimmering expanse of the Channel.

The leading vessel of the Newhaven force almost missed it altogether. But, mercifully, at that moment a cloud obscured the moon. With barely a second to spare, the entrance to the first of the channels being swept through the enemy mine-fields was sighted. It it hadn't been, all the Newhaven force would have had no choice but to take an incredible risk and press on through the minefields regardless. Later that night, this was precisely what the gunboat, *Locust*, had to do.

For the sea-borne part of Operation Jubilee had been timed to the very last split-second. All the assault forces must arrive off Dieppe at zero hour. No leeway was allowed for casting around to find the swept channels. They were either found, or they weren't, but in either event the ships went through without slackening speed.

Ten minutes after nine o'clock, the chief infantry landing ship, the *Princess Astrid*, cleared the Portsmouth boom ahead of the main body of the force. Behind her came the headquarters ship, *Calpe*, which was to be the nerve-centre of the entire operation. Behind *Calpe* were the destroyers *Albrighton*, *Bleasdale*, *Berkeley* and *Garth*. At half-past nine, every ship of the vast flotilla, big and small, two hundred and fifty of them, was at sea, and heading for the twin open-ings to the channels being swept through the minefields. The harbours of Newhaven, Shoreham, Southampton and Ports-mouth were empty. France lay ahead – destination Dieppe!

At Number Eleven Group Headquarters, the Combined Operations' Planning Staff talked tensely and waited, and chain-smoked. Radio silence blanketed the whole operation until zero hour. Once the ships were at sea, the die was cast for good or for ill.

In his office in South Kensington Felix Fenner paced the floor, chain-smoked his noxious Egyptian cigarettes, and waited too.

Richard Quintain, in France, the man on whom so much depended, did neither. He was far too busy. He couldn't wait. And, as for chain-smoking, he just hadn't the time.

*

Some few minutes after five o'clock that afternoon the Renault van had not been far from its objective – the rendezvous close to the E-boat base at Le Treport.

At six it would have been very, very much nearer – despite the devious route Quintain was having it take for safety's sake. Unfortunately, between five and six, a fan-belt snapped.

Consequently, at seven o'clock, there were still twelve kilometres to cover to reach the rendezvous with the Frenchmen who would take delivery of the explosive, position it, and detonate it. And those twelve kilometres had to be covered in one hundred and ten minutes. Two hours at the very most.

An easy task?

It would have been if there had been no such thing as a seven o'clock curfew along the German West Wall.

As it was, the Renault van could no longer be used with safety. To drive the noisy, rattling, smoking vehicle along quiet, restricted roads after curfew hour would have been madness. Armed Germans would have descended upon it like angry hornets. There was only one thing left to do.

And this was to go forward on foot; all of them together – Louis-Hercule, and Guillaume, and Rene, and Paul, and Quintain himself. Go forward like pack-animals with the explosive strapped to their backs, and be quiet, be stealthy, be careful, take no chances – and hope to cover the distance to the rendezvous in the time allowed them.

Twelve kilometres – seven and a half miles – in something less than two hours. Could they do it?

Quintain brushed the question aside. They had to do it! They had to reach the rendezvous – and reach it in time. He could not think of failure. Sweating, stumbling under their heavy loads, cursing, and quickly stifling the sounds, the men and the one woman struck forward.

And each carried enough explosive to flatten at least a quarter of a fair-sized town. Each carried detonators which, being old and unstable, might set off the explosive suddenly, ahead of time, and without any warning at all.

All of them, the men and the woman, were bowed down under a weight of possible, imminent death.

Meanwhile, on the outskirts of Le Treport, the French civilian saboteurs who had arrived at the rendezvous on edge and early, waited with mounting nervous impatience, and wondered if the high-explosive they needed for their assignment would evercome. One thing was certain; they could not, they dared not, wait long.

*

They could not wait long, these civilian workers from the E-boat base, and Quintain well knew it.

They would grant him a few minutes' leeway, no more. For the Germans were in the habit of making surprise spot-checks on the whereabouts of their French civilian labourers after curfew.

The deadly load of high-explosive had to be delivered on time, Quintain knew, so that the men who would use it could smuggle it into the base on time. Everything had to run like clockwork, or it would not run at all.

The explosive had to be delivered at the prearranged time, or weeks of preparation would all go for nothing. And Quintain's own efforts would all go for nothing.

Nor was this all.

Ten thousand times worse was the fact that the lives of many brave men would be placed in the direst jeopardy as a result. Canadians would scud in their landing craft through the false dawn . . . straight into hell.

Quintain tongue-lashed his companions forward.

Twice they had to crouch in ditches as German transport roared along the road. Once Louis-Hercule, slipping under his load, faltering in his age, very nearly brought down the fury of a passing patrol on their heads. Another time, the

116

young Paul coughed loudly at an awkward moment, and would have gone on coughing, too, if Quintain had not clamped an iron hand over his mouth to silence him.

Nevertheless, somehow they got through to the rendezvous. Somehow, by sheer force of personality, Quintain kept them going onward under their heavy loads.

And it was not his personality alone which kept them going and which brought them to a safe conclusion to their back-breaking trek. It was his care and caution and watchfulness, too. He never relaxed for an instant.

There was a traitor amongst them. Quintain did not forget that terrible fact. There was a traitor whose machinations he had to watch for, and counter, and guard against all the time.

The traitor had worked stealthily against Quintain from the first and, before his arrival at Gournay-en-Bray, against Gerard Heller.

Gerard had died in a Rouen gutter – shot down, running. So had the traitor initially triumphed. And many members of the Gournay-en-Bray maquis had been hounded to their deaths in the days which had followed. As a force, this particular maquis had well-nigh ceased to exist. The traitor had been highly successful.

But then Quintain had been sent to take Gerard's place with urgent plans for a 'special operation', and the traitor had had to go to work again, plotting, scheming, and doing everything possible to discover what this 'special operation' could be and to thwart it – working hand-in-hand with the Germans all the way.

And Quintain knew that even at this eleventh hour the traitor would seize any chance to bring the whole of the "special operation" down in ruins. This was why he was unceasingly vigilant.

As a result, the high-explosive was delivered – and exactly on time. And the Germans manning their West Wall remained unaware that it had been delivered. None of this was easy, but it had been accomplished.

At the rendezvous, shadowy figures rose out of the ground. A whispered conversation took place. Then heavy loads were transferred to new and willing backs, and with a whispered '*Bon Chance*! Good Luck!' Quintain and his companions started on the way they had come.

But still Quintain was vigilant. Still he did not, dared not, relax. Still he took no chances at all. He watched his tight little group like a hawk.

The high-explosive and detonators were safely in the hands of the men who could use them, but his mission was not completed – not yet. The traitor remained, ready, willing and able to bring the Germans down on them.

And that traitor had to be neutralized – permanently.

CHAPTER FIFTEEN

A WOOD spread its deep, dark seclusion over several miles of countryside half-way back along the road to where they had left the green Renault van.

Quintain drew his companions into its comparative safety.

They were, in the main, unwilling to accompany him into the wood. Paul was impatient to get out of the area. Guillaume and Rene were, too. All had gathered that, for them, the 'special operation' had ended with the safe delivery of the high explosive and detonators. Other men were about to demolish something of supreme importance to the enemy. The Germans would be outraged. Why dawdle in a restricted area under their very noses?

"The whole countryside around here is thick with the Boche!" Paul grumbled in a guttural growl. "We've done what we came to do – now let's get out before the high-explosive goes up and we're caught!"

Louis-Hercule was grumbling, too, but for another reason. "Why did we have to hand over the last part of the operation to somebody else, Damned errand boys, that's all we've been on this job!"

Marianne said quietly to Quintain: "Why have you brought us here?"

They were deep in the wood now.

"That's it! Why have you brought us here, what are we hanging about for? We ought to get the hell out of the area!"

Young Paul was eager to be somewhere else. He reminded Quintain – and it was an unfortunate comparison – of a man who had a pressing appointment with someone.

The traitor would be eager for a chance of passing on what he knew to the Germans even at this very late hour ...

Quintain spoke then, and spoke harshly, answering Paul and all the others.

"There's a traitor amongst us," he said. "That's why I have brought you here. We are all alone in the quiet and the dark to name names, and to see justice done!"

*

Louis-Hercule sounded aghast. "A traitor?" he echoed. "Are you sure?"

But then he answered the question himself.

"You must be sure! Of course you are sure!" The words came out of the old bull of Gournay-en-Bray in a growl and he swung round and slammed out an accusing finger. "And there he stands!"

Louis-Hercule's accusing finger pointed at Paul.

"No!" the young man got out. "No!"

But the others shrank away from him, and Louis-Hercule shouted him down. "You are the traitor! You! It is something I have suspected for a long time. Now everything is explained. The ambush, and before the ambush –"

"The traitor was certainly working before the ambush," Quintain said grimly. "Oh, yes."

"Fascist pig!" Louis-Hercule bellowed at Paul, crouching as if to spring upon the Alsatian. "*Saligaud*! Swine!"

Marianne tried to say something – tried to intervene – but Rene, small black eyes black with malevolence rounded on her.

"You'll keep out of this, if you know what's good for you! They were our comrades this rat betrayed. You'd better mind your own business!"

"But I am no traitor!" Paul protested. And, protesting his innocence, his guttural, Alsatian accent sounded thicker than ever before.

"Just listen to him!" Rene sneered, and spat into Paul's face.

The young man swung furiously at Rene, only to be stopped by the levelled Sten gun which slammed into his back, Guillaume behind it.

"Just one more move – go on, try it –!"

It was an evil invitation.

"Recall how he spoke to that Gestapo agent?"

"He disappeared before we set out in the van –"

"They were pigeons he kept in that wood –"

"For God's sake stop!" Paul shouted, but they were closing in on him now, with murder bright in their eyes.

"You've got to stop! You've got to give me a chance to explain!"

"You've done all the explaining you're going to do! What do you want to explain? And who to? The Germans?"

"Kill him!"

"Shoot him now!"

"Crucify him!" Louis-Hercule growled, and his eyes were black with hatred. "That's what we did with traitors and turncoats at Verdun. Crucify him!"

"Now, wait a minute –" It was Quintain speaking now. "The traitor must be executed humanely."

"Humanely!" sneered Rene. "They were our comrades that this one betrayed to the Gestapo. And did the Gestapo treat our comrades humanely? I wonder –"

"One of the men the traitor sold was an English agent," Quintain retorted.

The angry voices rose in fury.

"I command here!" Quintain said flatly. "It comes back to that! I command here until my work is done, and I will have the last word!"

There was a taut silence.

Then the sound came rushing back as Paul almost gabbled, "You've got to believe me! You must believe me –"

"*Ta bouche!*" snarled Louis-Hercule.

"All of you are making a terrible mistake!" Marianne cried, but her voice was lost.

"Silence!" roared Quintain, and quiet descended once more.

"I still command here!" Quintain declared grimly, "and we will do this my way." He turned his head to look at them all in turn. "You must accept my word that the traitor was responsible for the deaths of your comrades at German hands—"

"We do accept your word!"

"And you must believe that the traitor was responsible for the ambush on the road to Rouen and—" Quintain uttered the words lingeringly "—for other attempts to kill us all."

"We accept all of that!"

"He would have drawn attention to us as we carried our load along the road to the rendezvous—"

"But you stopped him! How is your cough now, eh, Paul?"

"Be quiet!" Quintain commanded.

Then he said: "I have listed the traitor's crimes. Now what should be the traitor's punishment? *Marianne*?"

The name snapped out like a whiplash. And, falteringly, she answered in a very small voice: "You're making a terrible mistake—"

"Answer me! What should be the traitor's punishment?"

"For the crimes you have named, death, but—"

"Death," Quintain repeated.

Marianne stared at him through suddenly terrified eyes.

"And you, Louis-Hercule, what do you say?"

"I still say crucify him! Death!" the old bull growled back.

"Rene?"

"*Death!*"

"Guillaume?"

"*Death!*"

"And . . . Paul . . ." Quintain said softly, "what do you say?"

122

"I say I am innocent! You must know that I am innocent! I –"

He stopped short as Rene struck him viciously across the mouth. "Silence, you bastard!"

"Give me your revolver," Quintain said to Louis-Hercule, and held out his hand for it.

Louis-Hercule passed the weapon over.

"Is it loaded?"

"Of course," the old bull confirmed grimly.

Quintain raised it.

"Then, in the name of France and her allies, I execute the sentence you have all just laid on the traitor." His knuckle was white as his finger tightened on the trigger. Paul stood up very straight.

"*Vive la France!*" he croaked, and awaited the bullet.

Quintain fired.

But, firing, he wheeled. And it was not Paul who fell with a bullet straight through his head between his eyes.

It was Louis-Hercule, the old bull of Gournay-en-Bray, the hero of Verdun.

He bellowed like a stricken animal – dead even as he cried.

He crashed on to his face.

Somewhere, far off, a cockerel crowed.

*

Quintain and Marianne stood in the still damp darkness on the edge of the wood. The moon was down, and they were alone. The others had gone.

"So it's all over," Marianne said softly, breaking the silence which lay between them.

"All over?" Quintain echoed quietly. "No, I don't think so. Not really. One phase has ended, that's all. For the moment our work here is done. But perhaps sometime soon we may return. Meantime, another phase – a greater phase – is about to begin."

He looked towards Le Treport, eyes probing the darkness, waiting . . .

"Who will lead them now?" Marianne asked. She was thinking of the men who had gone from them; the men of the Gournay-en-Bray maquis.

Quintain shrugged. "Rene, perhaps. Certainly not Paul. He was never forceful enough. Perhaps Rene."

"Paul had his suspicions of Louis-Hercule, you know," Marianne said. "He confided in me."

"So that's what you were always talking about so quietly and secretively together!"

Marianne said: "He thought that Louis-Hercule had a transmitter hidden in the farmhouse. He was almost certain he was in contact with the Germans –"

"He was right," Quintain said. "And he might have proved it himself if he'd been a little more forceful. *I* found Louis-Hercule's transmitter."

"You found it?" Marianne echoed. "When?"

"The night we arrived. I wasn't looking for it – nothing like that. I just came across it when I was taking a look over the farmhouse. I happened to knock against a wall and it sounded hollow, so –" he shrugged "– I investigated. There was a concealed cupboard –"

"And you found Louis-Hercule's transmitter! As long ago as that you knew he was working for the Germans!"

Quintain smiled somewhat wryly. "As long ago as that? It's only a matter of forty-eight hours ago."

"It seems longer," Marianne said, and it was true. Then she said: "But you knew this then?"

"I only knew that Louis-Hercule had a transmitter. It didn't mean that he was working hand-in-hand with the Germans. At least – not necessarily. I didn't know *that* fact for certain until I was taken to Gestapo Headquarters. There, on Anna Heyster's desk, I saw something. It fell on

124

the floor when she offered me a cigarette from a box. She pushed the box towards me, and this small, square bakelite crystal fell on the floor."

Marianne frowned. "A bakelite *crystal*?"

"One of those things that looks like a two-pin plug," Quintain explained. "You've used them – or seen them at least."

"A frequency crystal?"

"For V.H.F. use. Yes. That was what fell on the floor when Anna Heyster moved this cigarette box. I picked it up. And it was marked with its frequency in megacycles, as they all are. It was the same frequency I'd seen marked on the crystal in Louis-Hercule's transmitter. That clinched it for me – that, and all the other things which had happened, or were to happen, later."

"But why did Louis-Hercule turn traitor?" Marianne said rather helplessly. "That's what I can't understand! Why him, of all people? He was one of the heroes of Verdun –"

"I suppose he turned traitor because the France he believed in had collapsed," Quintain said slowly. "Or 'decayed', he would probably have said. It rotted from within. He can't have had much sympathy with the politicians who governed France between the wars –"

"These are reasons for a Frenchman to join forces with the hated Germans?"

"I suppose he looked for some sort of new order," Quintain said slowly. "An honourable order."

"Would he find it fighting on the side of his country's conquerors?"

"You made the point that he was one of the 'heroes' of Verdun," Quintain said. "Well, who was *his* hero? Can't we guess? Remember who led the French at Verdun?"

"Marshal Petain."

"Exactly. And whatever the old Marshal did would be what old Louis-Hercule would want to do too."

There Quintain stopped. For the event he had been waiting for had come to pass.

Light suddenly blazed across the western horizon. Light which soared upwards and outwards. Light which hurt the eyes just to look at it.

Marianne cried: "They've done it! They've done it!"

The next instant a muttering began. It was a muttering in a low register which swiftly increased in volume.

The earth shook beneath their feet as Quintain and Marianne stood there on the edge of the wood. The trees above them began to sway and dip in a sudden wind which blasted up to gale force, and then was as suddenly gone.

The E-boat pens at Le Treport were suddenly gone, too.

CHAPTER SIXTEEN

EMERGING from the German-laid minefield before the French coast in that early morning of Wednesday, August the nineteenth, nineteen forty-two, the two hundred and fifty-two ships of the assault flotilla moved at once into their positions for the attack.

The main obstacle of the night lay behind them. France lay ahead, invisible in the darkness. France – and Dieppe.

The ships fanned out over the sea. It was smooth, like a mill-pond. The ships took up station in thirteen groups.

Thirteen.

The order of battle called for landings at nine points. At Berneval and Belleville-sur-Mer on the left flank, at Puys on the inner left, on the east and west beaches of Dieppe itself in the centre, and at Pourville and Vesterival, Varengeville-sur-Mer and Quiberville on the right.

British Commandos were to land at Berneval and Belleville and at Quiberville, Vasterival and Varengeville-sur Mer; Number Three Commando on the left, Number Four on the right. All the other landings were to be made by Canadian regiments.

Fifty U.S. Rangers, the American equivalent of the British Commandos, were being carried on the operation to acquire battle experience.

The ships, in their predetermined groups, sailed on towards the shore.

At half-past two there came a tremendous flash, brighter than lightning. It lit up the whole eastern horizon. It was followed by a rumbling – a long-drawn-out explosion. Then – nothing.

On the headquarters ship, *Calpe*, officers looked at one another. *Le Treport . . . the E-boat pens*. Only time would tell.

At five minutes to three, the point of no return had been reached. All ships were in preordained positions exactly on time. The wireless silence had remained unbroken. There were no enemy aircraft overhead. The radar screens were full of outlines of the assault flotilla – nothing else.

At three o'clock the infantry landing ships began to put their assault craft into the water. The naval escorts, destroyers, torpedo-boats and gunboats, manoeuvred to lead them in to the waiting beaches.

*

Forty-five minutes later at fifteen minutes to four, with a full hour to go before zero, and the French coast eight miles ahead, S.G.B.5, the steam gunboat spearheading Group Five's attack, was leading in Number Three Commando at a steady nine-and-a-half knots towards the beaches of Berneval and Belleville-sur-Mer. Commander D.B. Wyburd was on the bridge.

At fifteen minutes to four the sea was slight and the wind was freshening from the west. The darkness was intense. The silence was almost complete.

Behind S.G.B.5 came the landing craft carrying the Commando. Out on the flanks of the group, somewhere in the darkness, steamed the destroyers Brocklesby and Slazak. Nearer to the assault craft, bringing up the rear of the group, were additional escorts, a motor launch and a flak landing craft.

At fourteen minutes to four, nothing had changed. Sixty seconds went by. And then – at thirteen minutes to four – it happened!

One moment Commander Wyburd was staring ahead into the darkness and seeing nothing. In the next, he saw a shape looking up fast on his port bow. It was a shape that was a ship.

A star-shell burst overhead. Five ships stood in an arc across the gunboat's bows. Everything happened at once.

The gunboat's forward guns blazed as concentrated fire raked her fore and aft, wrecking the wireless gear in the first second. The gunboat continued to steam dead ahead at exactly nine and a half knots. For the next thirteen minutes S.G.B.5 engaged an enemy superior in everything except, perhaps, in courage.

She engaged an enemy which five times battered her boilers with direct hits, silenced her guns, and strewed half her crew wounded and bleeding across the decks.

All this time there was no sign of S.G.B.5's escorting destroyers Brocklesby and Slazak.

Meanwhile, the flak landing ship, under the command of Lieutenant A. D. Fear, stormed into the battle and engaged the enemy with her twin four-inch guns to such effect that she had one enemy ship on fire and another one sinking before any guns were brought to bear upon her.

The enemy then made off – five armed trawlers bound for Dieppe. They left behind them a disabled gunboat wallowing in the water, a flak landing ship with its fire-control shot away, and five landing craft.

The rest had scattered.

Where they had gone, nobody knew. Where the motor-launch had gone, nobody knew. Where the destroyers Brocklesby and Slazak had gone, nobody knew. Nor had they the means to find out.

Group Five was without any communications equipment of any sort. It had all been destroyed. As a fighting force, Group Five had ceased to exist. It was, the Commander of Number Three Commando decided, impossible and worse than useless to take his force ashore on the beaches of Berneval and Belleville, as planned.

Somehow, this fact had to be reported to the headquarters ship, *Calpe*.

One of the five remaining five landing craft was cleared of men. This took the commanding officer of Number Three Commando and Wyburd in search of the *Calpe*. The remaining four landing craft stood by to tow the crippled steam gunboat all the way back to England. The time was now five minutes to five.

It was five minutes after the planned time of the assault on the left-flank beaches, and the men who should have made that assault were . . . where?

Most of them were scattered. There was no doubt of that. But, unbeknown to the officers bearing these grim tidings to the *Calpe*, a landing on the left flank *had* been made. And exactly at the time predetermined.

Seventeen men and three officers of Number Six Troop, Number Three Commando, had got ashore at Belleville. And their resolve was quite clear and straightforward.

During the battle with the German trawlers they had made off into the night, but not out of cowardice. They had gone ahead simply to carry out their orders.

They landed at Belleville without encountering any opposition. They planned, the twenty of them, to do their damnedest to fulfil the task which had been allotted to t' :m in the order of battle.

This was to attack, and to silence, the Goebbels battery of four 5.9 inch guns – one of the batteries defending Dieppe.

The twenty commandos struck up from the beach to get to grips with the Goebbels battery and its garrison of more than two hundred men.

*

Day was almost turned back into night.

There was thick black smoke over Dieppe.

Black, man-made smoke which veiled ten miles of coastline in shifting, choking clouds, polluting the air of the morning.

And through this smoke fighters and fighter-bombers of the R.A.F screamed earthward to hit their ground targets again and again, whilst above, below them, and on either side, the sky was filled with the hurtling fragments of a thousand exploding shells. Flame erupted skywards, turning the rags of smoke a bloody red.

Focke-Wulf 190's streaked out of the hazy sun like bitter arrows. A Boston bomber cartwheeled out of the smoke and exploded on impact with the shell-torn sea. On the beaches beneath the smoke, nearly five thousand men fought for a foothold on the sliding, blood-slimed stones.

Again and again they charged the German defences. The bodies of dead comrades were soft and yielding, bleeding bridges across the morass of the wire, and those who charged now, and fell gaping-mouthed, were stepping stones for others coming after.

Mounting, furious thunder filled the air of the morning. High explosive shells fired by the British warships standing out to sea tore the heart out of the hotels along Dieppe's Boulevard de Verdun. More bombs rained down – British and German.

Flanking Wehrmacht batteries laid a barrage on the beaches and for a thousand yards out to sea. Tank-landing craft were opened up like sardine cans. The sea frothed and boiled red. Singing high above the tumult of explosions, like the wind plucking a million telephone wires at once, machine-guns twittered obscenely a serenade to death and destruction.

As the Canadian troops on the beaches tried again and again to break through the German defences and enter the town, Churchill tanks were landed behind them, in support.

There were twenty-eight Churchill tanks.

More than half of them had their tracks blown off before

they had even begun to charge upwards out of the surf and across the shell-flayed shingle. But at least five survived to plough through the enemy wire and scale the fortified seawall beyond. Four of the five got into the town.

After them and around them and behind them, some small groups of Canadians got off the beaches too. The strongly defended Casino to the west of Dieppe was carried by assault, and isolated Canadian patrols ranged through the entire German defence system, creating havoc wherever they could.

The main body of the five thousand men committed to the assault, however, did not get off the beaches. They stayed there, and fought there, and died there. For them, there was no escape.

The gaps torn in their defence wall by the tanks were were quickly blanketed by the Germans with a mounting barrage of shells.

The shingle beaches of Dieppe became a killing ground. It was that from then on until the end.

CHAPTER SEVENTEEN

THE fierce assault planned against the Goebbels battery at Belleville, on the left, had been reduced by ill-luck and a chance encounter with five armed trawlers to little more than a courageous foray by twenty foolhardy men, but on the right the two hundred and fifty members of Lord Lovat's Number Four Commando were going in to hit their target – the Hess battery – exactly as planned.

The flanking batteries – Goebbels, Rommel and Hess – east and west of Dieppe, dominated the sea and the beaches in the centre, where the main Canadian landings would be made. If the batteries were permitted unlimited, uninhibited freedom of fire, the main assault must, inevitably, suffer terrible casualties.

It was this knowledge which had spurred on the twenty men of Number Three Commando to make their landing at Belleville. The same urgent intelligence was imprinted upon the minds of all the members of Number Four Commando now.

The time was fifteen minutes to five. The darkness was lightening towards nautical twilight and the dawn. Tense in their landing craft, the commandos began to close the silent, empty beaches of Vasterival and Quiberville.

There was no sign whatsoever of any enemy activity.

In exactly four hundred and eighty seconds, cannon-firing Spitfires would attack the Pointe d'Ailly light, the lighthouse high on the headland west of Vasterival which served the Hess Battery as an observation post. This would create a diversion, and the commandos were ready to take full advantage of it. Scudding in through the thin mist which covered the water beneath the tall cliffs, driving straight for their appointed beaches under the wheeling wings of roaring aircraft, the commandos' ramps would go down on shingle not more than thirty seconds after the Spitfires' attack began.

The men racing ashore at Vasterival, under Major D. Mills Roberts, would make a frontal assault on the Hess battery. Those landing at Quiberville, a mile away, under the direct command of their colonel, Lord Lovat, would cut inland to fall upon the battery from the rear.

Fourteen minutes after the Spitfires attacked the light, Number Four Commando should be well on its way to attaining its objective and the bombardment of Dieppe itself would begin. Fifteen minutes after that, the first Canadian troops would hit the beaches in the centre.

*

The seconds ticked relentlessly away. The enemy coast lay dark and silent ahead. Three miles behind the commando landing craft, a vast concourse of little ships, deployed in a wide arc, drove in towards the central beaches at a steady ten knots.

The Point d'Ailly light, high on its headland flashed its normal characteristic. The enemy seemed to be completely unaware of the armada approaching his shore. The distance between the commando landing craft and their appointed beaches narrowed.

Men felt cold now. Cold with the sudden chill which is the prelude to any violent action.

Still their craft drove on.

And then, eerily, wailing at them over the water, there came the sound of air-raid sirens from the shore. The Spitfires were coming. Zero hour was near.

Heard at first as a far-off drone – a small sound, almost drowned by the wailing sirens, but growing louder, louder – two aircraft suddenly thunderbolted out of the twilit sky to blast the Point d'Ailly light absolutely on schedule.

And, absolutely on schedule, at Vasterival and Quiber-ville, the commando landing craft went in.

*

Lord Lovat's landing was made in two waves – with recision.

At the instant of the touchdown, the first wave, led by Lieutenant Veasey, leapt for the shore.

Disdaining cover, fully aware that they had only one minute – or two at the most – won for them by superb timing and tactical surprise, before the enemy hit back, and hit back hard, Veasey and his men charged across open shingle or the dark line of the cliffs.

As warning star-shells alerted the enemy on the cliff-top, Veasey and his men thrust tubular steel ladders against the cliffs and scaled them. They scaled them so quickly that they were upon the forward positions of the enemy before a single shot had been fired to stop them.

Grenades flung with terrible accuracy hurled the enemy out of cover. Two pill-boxes were over-run and overwhelmed in as many seconds.

It was part of Veasey's task to cut communications, and to this end, Trooper Finney, one of his men, had detached himself from the rest of the troop as the cliff-top was reached. Now he dived for the nearest telegraph pole and began to swarm up it. But the enemy was now so alert that Finney came under machine-gun fire before he had climbed three feet.

Bullets tore the pole to splinters almost beneath his hands. Still he went on climbing, to straddle the crossbars at the top of the pole and calmly shear through the wires before sliding down again unscathed

Veasey's men deployed then, to harry the enemy with all their power. Behind and below them, on the beaches, the second wave of commandos had landed.

The second wave touched down close to the estuary of

the Saane river, where the shingle gives way to sand. The line of the beach is spaced by wooden groynes here and, at the moment of touchdown, it seemed as if the whole world exploded as a hail of German mortar bombs came down on the groynes and the deep belts of wire between them.

The first men to reach the wire died as they tried to bridge it with rabbit netting. Machine-guns reinforced the mortars now. But in the face of a storm of fire, Lovat rushed the wire with his main force and, using the bodies of the men who had died as bridges, got safely across without another casualty.

The landing craft which had brought the commandos now drew out to sea. But for the dead, Quiberville beach was deserted. Disengaging from the enemy, Lovat and his men struck quickly along the bank of the Saane river and gained the cover of Blancmenil wood, which edged the rear of the Hess battery.

*

Lord Lovat had encountered and overcome fierce enemy opposition to his landing. At Vasterival Major Mills Roberts encountered none. He and his men got ashore on a boulder-strewn beach and, timing the explosion to the last of the cannon-firing Spitfires' attack on the lighthouse, blasted a way through the German wire on the beach to reach the cliff-top in under five minutes.

Here Major Mills Roberts divided his forces. While Lieutenant Style, with one troop, penetrated the village of Varengeville less than a quarter of a mile inland, Mills Roberts himself moved very fast with a mortar section to reach the cover of the woods beyond – the woods which ended barely two hundred yards from the Hess battery wire.

Not a single shot had yet been fired. The landings seemed to have passed off entirely unnoticed by the enemy.

And this was confirmed by Lieutenant Style's experience in Varengeville. He and his men arrived in the village un challenged by a single sentry and were able to move, quietly and systematically, from house to house, dealing with the German soldiers billeted in the village and reassuring the French civilians they startled along the way. In less than ten minutes, and in near-silence, all the Germans in the village had been accounted for, and a vital line of retreat to the beach bridgehead secured. Lieutenant Style then rejoined Mills Roberts. Together with their men they worked their way through the wood until the forward boundary was reached.

They had moved quickly.

It was ten minutes past five.

*

It was ten minutes past five and, across the sea, out of the grey northern sky, the low murmur of aircraft engines swelled to a roar as Bostons and Blenheims, Spitfires and Hurricanes swooped upon Dieppe.

The brief preliminary bombardment of the town began.

One thousand yards out to sea, keeping careful station, the great host of landing barges and little ships which bore the Canadians who would make the main assault, drove in towards the land. The Bostons and Blenheims screamed over them almost at mast-height.

And then the destroyer escorts opened fire, punching holes through the smoke screens the aircraft were laying, and setting the whole of the promenade ablaze.

Bombs rained down on the East headland. Flame leapt, answering, upwards. Tracer drew dotted lines in orange light across the sky. Anti-aircraft batteries thudded.

The shallow curve of the enemy coastline erupted into a hell of fire and screaming metal, whining aircraft, the deadly shuffle of shells passing overhead, and the staccato rattle of machine-guns sounding like sticks being drawn across half-a-hundred corrugated roofs.

Still the landing craft moved towards the beaches. Eight hundred yards now. Now seven hundred. Now six, five, four, three, two –

At two hundred yards three red Very lights soared from the leading craft to lift the destroyers' barrage clean across the town. More than twenty hotels and tall houses burned on the Boulevard de Verdun.

As the barrage lifted, support landing craft poured smoke-shells on the fringes of the sea. The distance narrowed. Through the smoke the leading assault craft emerged to drop their ramps on the beach.

And then the enemy guns roared out. All the enemy guns, in a furious hideous bellow. It was almost as though the German gunners had been holding the greater part of their fire-power especially for this moment.

The foreshore erupted. The sea boiled. Between the beach and the town stood the massive, heavily fortified sea wall, a thing of masonry and concrete ten feet high and fifteen hundred yards long.

The Royal Hamiltons of Canada charged out of their landing craft into a hail of death. They were boxed in on all sides by screaming steel. They fought for a foothold on the shingle and the stones.

*

Numbers Three and Four Commando had been assigned the task of dealing with the Goebbels battery and the Hess battery, and to the Royal Regiment of Canada had gone the job of silencing the battery which remained.

The Rommel battery. The heaviest of the three.

The Royals were to land at Puits and destroy this. They were also to attack the fortified East headland, Bismarck, above Dieppe.

But the Royals were late.

They had lost thirty vital minutes forming up into a flotilla after clearing the German minefields at half-past three. They had formed up behind the wrong gunboat and half an hour had gone by before they had found the right one.

Three thousand six hundred terribly wasted seconds.

They had been unable to regain all this time. Try as they might, they were still late when they approached the narrow channel which leads to the sheltered beach at Puits – their landfall.

They were only seventeen minutes late then – but it was enough.

An hour before, the harbour light at Dieppe had flashed interrogation signals at their flotilla. The signals had had to be left unanswered. Thereafter, all the way in to their appointed beach, a German searchlight played steadily upon the Royals' craft. There was no evading its beam, and there was no going back. The Royals had accepted a task, and it was an important one. It was one of supreme importance to the safety of their compatriots on the beaches in the centre. They must at least try to silence the Rommel battery and attack the Bismarck headland. They must see this job through to the end.

So the landing craft came on without pause, and the searchlight's beam grew brighter and brighter. And men's faces were plainly visible to one another in the boats. Tight-lipped faces. Grim faces. The distance between the ships and the shore steadily narrowed.

The craft came to the channel leading through shelved rocks to the beach, and entered it. The cliffs reached up to enclose them on either side. And still, for one long, final moment, the searchlight played on them.

And then, as the flotilla came on through the Channel, the first enemy bullets met them. Snipers' bullets from well-placed men firing on carefully-selected targets.

The Royals wearing badges of rank were shot down first. Then men carrying signals' equipment. Half the officers in the first wave were dead or dying before the ramps were down and the beach was reached. But this was only a prelude

139

to what was to follow – the Devil's *hors d'oeuvre* to a grisly feast of blood and death.

For, as the first wave of landing craft touched down on the shingle, all the enemy's guns were unleashed upon them. Heavy machine-guns, mortars, light anti-aircraft guns, anti-tank guns, and even howitzers firing over open sights carved bloody swathes through the men in the boats. From pill-boxes on the cliffs and from the cliff-tops the Germans fired straight down into the living, the dead, and the dying who choked the assault craft.

Still the officers who survived tried to rally their men. Bellowing in an effort to be heard above the roar of war and the cries of the wounded, they tried to break the Germans' grip upon the beach, and they led a dozen abortive charges on the sea-wall which, twelve feet high and of reinforced concrete crowned with barbed wire, embedded with pill-boxes at planned intervals, barred all escape from the reeking slaughterhouse of the Royals' landing.

From the pill-boxes embedded in the wall the hellish fire of heavy machine-guns and men were cut down before they had covered five yards towards them. Yet one man, Lieutenant Wedd, with members of A and B Companies being massacred at his heels, did reach the wall and, even though he reached it alone, he didn't hesitate.

He had located the concrete pill-box from which the most deadly and accurate stream of fire was pouring and now, gauging to the last split-second how long he had to live, he stood upright before it – there was no other way – and he silenced the pill-box by hurling a grenade through the firing-slit and killing every man inside it.

Then he, too, died. But his sacrifice had not been entirely in vain.

True, the rate of enemy fire on to the beach did not slacken perceptibly, but on Lieutenant Wedd's immediate left, a Captain Sinclair and a Lieutenant Patterson reached the wall unharmed with a Corporal Ellis. The men carried

Bangalore torpedoes between them and they made for the central steps, filled with wire, which split the wall and suggested a possible exit from the beach.

Lieutenant Patterson was dead before the Bangalore torpedoes could be exploded to breach the wire, and Captain Sinclair died immediately after waving Corporal Ellis to precede him through the gap the torpedoes made. No-one followed the corporal through. No-one could. There was an exit from the beach now, but no-one could reach it. The fury of the enemy fire increased in intensity.

In the channel, just off the beach, the landing craft which had brought the Royals here disdained the safety of the open sea and answered the enemy guns with their own. But nothing they could do relieved the pressure on the men on the beach nor made the German fire slacken for a moment so that they might make their escape from it.

Beyond the gap in the wire, in the shelter of some bushes, Corporal Ellis waited for some of his companions to join him. No-one came. He waited a long time.

Then, picking up his rifle, he left Puits and made his way inland to see what he could do alone against the enemy.

Behind him, on the extreme left, Lieutenant-Colonel Catto, the officer commanding the landing, managed with a sergeant, a forward observation officer of the destroyer, *Garth*, and eleven men to cut a way through the wire surmounting the wall.

Catto immediately led his men on an assault up the cliff and took the fortified houses on the cliff top. Then he led his men back to the beach to try and rally the others to attempt a break-through.

None was possible. The enemy had detected the gap he had cut in the wire and it was covered by heavy fire. The colonel could not reach the beach nor those of his men who still survived there.

Corporal Ellis was much . . . *luckier?*

After raiding the village of Puits and doing all that he

141

could do to harry the enemy single-handed, he returned the way he had come and pushed his way through the gap in the wire on the steps.

He found the beach silent and littered with dead. All firing had stopped now, and nothing moved.

There were perhaps, a hundred men alive on the beach at that moment – a hundred out of the five hundred and forty-three who had attempted the assault – but they all feigned death.

And from the sea-wall, and from the pill-boxes on the cliff and along the cliff-top, the Germans looked down, rifles and machine-guns ready, and searched the heaps of dead for any movement.

*

At Vasterival, Major Mills Roberts and his men were so close to the Hess battery that they could clearly hear the words of command given to the gunners.

Silently the major set up his mortar section, and Lieutenant Style took his troop forward, in cover, to positions from which they could pick off the enemy with the greatest of ease.

The battery had, by now, fired several salvos on the central beaches, but it was clear from scraps of conversation easily overheard that the enemy were as yet unaware of the full significance of the situation which faced them.

Major Mills Roberts glanced at his watch and bided his time.

Until ten minutes to six, the major waited and then, at his signal, his men fired as one with devastating effect.

The enemy was punched off-balance. The fire returned was erratic and wild. And only minutes later Troop Sergeant-Major Dunning, with Privates Dale and Horne and a two-inch mortar dealt the battery a body-blow.

They planted a mortar bomb on the cordite charges and shells brought up from the magazines and stacked behind the guns ready for action. There was a blinding white flash, a roar of mighty wind, and men were hurled through the air like twigs in a gale.

The Hess battery never fired again.

Out of the flaming inferno at the heart of the battery came the shrill screams of the burning as the garrison ran wild in an attempt to rescue the wounded, put out the flames, and save the guns. Into this scene of confusion Mills Roberts' men poured a hail of fire.

They had to keep the enemy off-balance and on the defensive. The battery, as a battery, had ceased to be of consequence, but it was garrisoned by over four hundred men, a force which could squash Mill Roberts' troops with ease if it were ever allowed to make the attempt.

So, until twenty minutes past six – when three white Very lights rose behind the battery to tell the major that Lord Lovat was in position and beginning his assault from the rear, Mills Roberts did all he could to hamper and demoralize the battery's garrison.

And then, seeing the Very lights, he withdrew through the woods, through the village, to the beach.

On the way back one of his men was killed by a German mortar-bomb, and Lieutenant Style was badly wounded in the leg. But this was the sum total of the damage inflicted on Mills Roberts' forces by the enemy.

He embarked his men as swiftly and as silently as they had landed. Their work was done.

*

The roar of the exploding cordite set off by Troop Sergeant-Major Dunning gladdened the hearts of Lovat's men as they took up their positions in the Hess battery's rear.

They were almost ready to make their own assault.

Six U.S. Rangers, practically all of the small American token force to get ashore, covered the commando's flanks.

Two American sergeants with an American corporal, Koons, had meanwhile gained entry to some nearby houses and climbed, unseen, on to rooftops overlooking the battery.

At quarter-past six, absolutely on time, cannon-firing fighters of the R.A.F. screamed down out of the sky on top of the battery to signal Lovat's assault.

The white Very lights were fired. Lovat and his men went in with bayonets fixed.

The cannon-firing fighters were being harrassed by Focke-Wulfe 190's now and, in shallow dives, they blasted the U.S. Rangers from their positions of vantage overlooking the battery. The Americans found themselves on the ground, but unhurt. Intoxicated by this discovery they lost no time in getting back to the rooftops and pouring a stream of fire into the battery. Corporal Koons was the first American soldier to kill a German in the war.

Meanwhile the enemy on the ground was fighting back, and hitting hard. Leading the charge of F Troop over open ground, Captain Pettiward and Lieutenant MacDonald were killed within split-seconds of each other, and Major Porteous leapt forward to head the troop. Wounded three times in as many seconds he held the lead as the enemy defence positions were overrun and their guns silenced.

Company Sergeant-Major Stockdale, simultaneously, was seen to be calmly firing from a sitting position, blasting the enemy with telling effect, and completely ignoring the fact that his left foot had just been blown off.

Other troops of the commando fared similarly. B Troop had had its casualties, but had swept like a scythe through the defences to the very heart of the battery. There German gunners were bayonetted beside their stricken guns. Only four of the enemy survived B Troop's assault. The rest died – or fled.

Barely ten minutes after Lovat had sent up the white signals to initiate his attack the last strong-points within the battery fell. At ten minutes to seven, F Troop blew up the five fifteen-centimetre guns on the central emplacements. A few moments later, Lance Corporal Skerry, working alone, blew up the sixth gun, used as an anti-aircraft defence, some distance away.

One last thing remained to be done before the commando quitted the scene. Swiftly the wounded were brought in and the bodies of the dead were collected. There was no time for a prolonged search. Eleven dead were found and twenty-two wounded.

The dead were laid gently down in a row on the scorched and blackened earth in the centre of the gun-site and, at a signal from Lord Lovat, the Union Jack was run up over them. Their comrades stood for a long moment in silent salute, and then turned away.

They did not leave the soil of France by the same way that they had come. The beaches at Quiberville were being watched very closely by the enemy whilst those at Vasterival, where Mills Roberts had landed, still were not.

Lovat and his men left France by the same beaches as Mills Roberts. They embarked without difficulty, covered by three assault craft and a motor gunboat. Thirteen men remained unaccounted for – missing presumed dead – but Number Four Commando left with all its wounded and without a single, further casualty.

*

At Puits, Captain Browne, the Forward Observation officer of the destroyer *Garth*, had succeeded in contacting his ship. He appealed for covering fire and, at twenty minutes to eight, at the same moment as a squadron of Hurricane fighter-bombers attacked the East headland, the *Garth* began to lob shells into the German positions. In the middle of this diversion, two assault landing craft came in through the narrow channel towards the littered beach.

All over the beach the dead lay in clusters. And near the

dead, feigning the same eternal sleep as their comrades, lay the living. But as the assault landing craft came in through the surf with their ramps down, the living got to their feet and rushed them. They overwhelmed the leading vessel by sheer weight of numbers. And into this clawing, terrible, scrambling mass of humanity the Germans fired and fired again.

The assault craft, its ramp still down, managed to drag itself back from the beach and fifty yards out to sea. And then a direct hit from a shell capsized it. There were great flurries in the water as machine-gun bullets took toll of those Royals who had tried to escape this way.

The second assault craft fared a little better. Many men were cut down before they reached it. The few who did got safely away.

All through the morning, hour after hour, while there was still hope that some living lingered among the dead on the beach at Puits, assault craft tried to make an entry through the narrow channel in the face of crippling fire.

In all, out of the twenty-seven officers and five hundred and sixteen men of the Royal Regiment of Canada who had landed, only three officers and fifty-seven men survived.

The Rommel battery fired uninterruptedly. The Bismarck headland remained in German hands.

*

The Hamiltons and the Essex Scottish had landed on the beaches in the centre and straightway encountered a murderous reception. The German fire-power brought to bear was tremendous. From a hundred unidentifiable points, a torrent of fire was unleashed upon the beach.

Overhead, fighters and fighter-bombers of the R.A.F. flew mission after mission against enemy strong-points, bombing, laying smoke, and harrying the Germans with cannon and machine-gun fire. On the ground the Hamiltons and the

Essex Scottish tried to storm the sea wall, secure the beach, and gain a foothold in the town beyond. Through flying spray and shell-torn surf, tank-landing craft came in to bring them the support of armour – all to no avail.

The tank-landing craft, trying to hit the beaches with their ramps down, were ungainly sitting-ducks and were hit time and time again. Men died in them, around them, and in front of them, like flies.

Of one group of seventy-one sappers trying to blast a way clear through the wire along the beach only nine survived the first moments of landing, and four of these were wounded. Of the twenty-four tank-landing craft which had negotiated the minefields early that morning only ten managed to land any tanks at all, and these put twenty-eight Churchills over their ramps. One of these was immediately drowned as it blundered forward into the sea out of its depth. Twenty more were swiftly knocked out by the German gun. Seven crossed the wall to the Esplanade where one was caught in a tank trap and its crew died fighting. Six shelled enemy positions along the sea-front and then penetrated the town.

None returned.

Nevertheless, the tanks' covering fire did enable some of the Hamiltons and Essex Scottish to get off the beach, and if more armour had been landed the story along the Dieppe waterfront might have been very different. But at six o'clock, as the smoke cleared from the East headland, the enemy played his trump card.

Guns whose existence had never even been suspected sent shell after shell screaming out of the mouths of the East Headland caves. All available destroyers turned their guns upon the headland in an effort to smash this new threat, but it was hopeless. The German guns, heavy 75s and 88s were invulnerable, and they enfiladed the approaches to the beach. They made the supply of reinforcing armour impossible.

In the absence of more tanks and more men the capture

of the beach was impossible too, and the whole of the plan for Operation Jubilee fell to the ground.

Still – the men on shore did the best they could. They fought and they died where they were and some, the luckier ones off the beach now with the help of the tanks which had landed, mounted an assault against the strongly fortified Casino, whilst others penetrated the town a short distance and members of the Royal Canadian Engineers set fire to warehouses near the tobacco factory.

This was the picture at nine o'clock.

Operation Jubilee had failed as a whole, though some parts of the plan had been amazingly successful.

Number Four Commando had carried out its appointed tasks with precision. Twenty officers and other ranks of Number Three Commando had tried and, landing at Berneval, had harried the Goebbels battery with such success that it hadn't fired a shell for the first one and a half hours of the main landings.

As for the rest, the dead lay in heaps on the beach at Puits and along the waterfront of Dieppe itself the Essex Scottish and the Hamiltons were fighting desperately to maintain themselves under steadily increasing enemy fire. The South Saskatchewan Regiment had landed at Pourville and was trying to take Quatre Vents Farm, an enemy stronghold. The Queens Own Cameron Highlanders were about two and a quarter miles inland striving to reach St. Aubin aerodrome.*

---

*A group of armed civilians fired on the Canadians, but it was not possible – even long afterwards – to ascertain who they were. Even the Germans never found out.

In Dieppe itself, few prisoners were taken. Surrendering Germans were killed. Only about 30 prisoners were taken on the entire operation, and brought back to England, and these were captured by No. 4 Commando in the course of its separate and distinct part of the operation, and by the crew of HMS *Brocklesby* after a brief engagement at sea.

C Company of the South Saskatchewan Regiment which had landed at Pourville spot on schedule at 04.52, from the first enjoyed almost

148

Some of the craft off the beaches were running out of fuel, and at least one of the destroyers had little ammunition left.

The Naval and Military Force Commanders aboard the Headquarters ship *Calpe* considered what must be done.

There was only one thing which could be done. Withdrawal had to be ordered. But withdrawal must be delayed at least two hours to give the Royal Air Force, on whose support an orderly evacuation must depend, time to adjust its complex schedules to give maximum assistance and provide a covering smoke-screen.

The battle, although lost, must go on for two hours more.

Evacuation was timed for eleven o'clock. The code-name assigned to it was – *Vanquish*.

complete surprise. Monsieur Sade, the owner of the Hotel la Terrace, was sleeping peacefully when he was awakened by a hubbub of noise. Seeing lights outside he called out to his guests: "What the hell are you doing with all those lights? You'll get us all into trouble."

"But, don't you know? The Tommies have landed. You'd better take shelter!"

Everyone rushed into the cellar.

M. Sade was not the only one taken by surprise. At the Maison Blanche, further along the beach, there'd been a party the previous evening, and a dozen or so German officers were sleeping off a very good time. They never woke. The invaders cut their throats or strangled them as they slept.

CHAPTER EIGHTEEN

AT Field Marshal von Rundstedt's headquarters the news of the assault came in a mounting flood beginning at a little after five in the morning and jamming the telephone exchanges by ten.

But always three lines were kept open.

Two of these lines ran directly to where the 10th Panzer Division and the SS Division *Adolf Hitler* were held poised and ready for action on the outskirts of the town.

The other telephone line led to the Supreme Headquarters of the Fuehrer himself.

At half-past ten, with the bulk of the Allied forces engaged in the operation known to still be unable to break out from the beaches, there was no doubt in Von Rundstedt's mind that whatever its objectives the enemy attack upon Dieppe had failed in almost every particular.

True, Commandos landing to the west of Dieppe before the main assault on the centre had obliterated a battery of heavy guns, and reports which had reached his headquarters during the early hours of the night had already told the Field Marshal that the destruction of the E-boat base at Le Treport had been absolute. But these were blows which, though savage, could be born with equanimity. Of the two, the loss of the E-boat base was the most serious.

On the other hand, after five and a half hours, the enemy had made little progress with the main assault on Dieppe itself and, with every passing minute, Von Rundstedt knew the chances of war became more and more heavily loaded in a defender's favour.

He had allowed the Dieppe garrison – mostly second-grade troops – to absorb all the shock of the assault until now, and his confidence in the sound sense of these tactics had not been misplaced.

Now, at this moment, at half-past ten in the morning, he decided that the time had come to force a new and much bloodier Dunkirk. Now he threw into the scales his fresh but battle-drilled divisions – the best troops he had.

The Panzers rolled into the town.

The SS Division marched.

Over the telephone line to his headquarters the Fuehrer, Adolf Hitler, was kept fully informed of what his Field Marshal was doing. Almost simultaneously, the first propaganda broadcasts put out by the B.B.C. and the Americans were monitored in Berlin. Translations of these broadcasts, together with a 'Most Secret' battle order captured early in the fighting at Dieppe, were placed before Hitler at the same time.

He read them. He read the opening words of the American news bulletin. It said: We and the British invade France.

On news-stands throughout the United States, banner headlines screamed: YANKS RAID DIEPPE!

Hitler already knew from the 'Most Secret' battle order that only fifty United States soldiers were involved in the entire operation.

He began to laugh.

He was still laughing when, some minutes later, a staff secretary was called to take his dictation of the first communique concerning the Raid on Dieppe, to be issued from his headquarters.

His laughter was echoed, throatily, by howitzers and the heavy guns of the Goebbels and Rommel batteries firing from the East Headland above Dieppe. On the beaches, and on the shingle, lapped by slow-moving waters, the first flower of Canadian manhood lay in bloody heaps.

At that moment over forty out of the fifty Americans assigned to the operation were nearing the shores of England without ever having effected a landing at Dieppe at all. They were returning to port.

Adolf Hitler's laughter would probably have been all the louder had he known that.

*

"But why did they come?" Hitler put the question to Field Marshal Keitel as they bent over battle-maps in the Operations Room of his headquarters. "Why did the British attempt an assault on Dieppe at all?"

He had his own answer ready. He didn't wait for Keitel to speak.

"They attempted to take Dieppe just to prove that it couldn't be done," he said. And he spoke with certainty.

Keitel stared at him.

Hitler flicked the monitored report of the British news broadcast with contemptuous fingers. "Not an invasion? Only a raid with limited objectives? What objectives? A dress rehearsal –! Really, can't they do better than that?"

Again his fingers trifled with the report. "All this they put out this morning – just before the assault was beginning. In other words, they were explaining failure before it happened! They were vague about their objectives. Did they really send five thousand men across the Channel just to blow up a few gun emplacements and hold a town for two or three hours? Their own people may believe them – they have to! But do we? I think not!"

He swung away from the maps and from Keitel. He began to pace the floor jerkily, his hands clasped behind his back, his head thrown forward, the famous forelock almost in his eyes.

"No, we don't have to believe them. We can imagine the truth. The Kremlin put pressure on Churchill. Roosevelt –" and he spat the name "– also put pressure on Churchill. Invade now. *Do* something! This was their cry. So he shows them – failure. He knows that if he came in strength today, or tomorrow, or the next day, we would annihilate his divisions. So he sends us only a few men . . . sacrifices."

He stopped pacing. His head jutted forward as he turned. He spoke like an oracle.

"This must be the truth about Dieppe. This must have been an assault planned with failure in mind. One can reach no other conclusion."

*

At ten o'clock that morning Quintain and Marianne entered Dieppe.

They entered the town from the west. They had spent many hours along the way and they were very tired.

They were, in fact, more than tired. They were weary to the point of exhaustion, and sick at heart. For they had witnessed many terrible sights along the way.

They had seen haunting things which would stay with them for as long as they lived: acts of butchery and savage slaughter, and deeds of hopeless courage and throat-catching heroism which brought tears to the eyes. They had seen ships coming in from the sea; little ships bearing men into the mouths of the enemy guns like a sacrifice.

Now they had reached Dieppe.

Above them enemy bombers roared loud and low towards the sea. Spitfires and Hurricanes and Focke-Wulfe 190s screamed over the town, and added the savage rattle of guns to the symphony of hate now rising to its furious crescendo along the waterfront.

Buildings were burning all around. German soldiers were in the streets. Soldiers who, on one occasion, coming upon Quintain and Marianne, took them for French civilians and brusquely ordered them into the nearest house.

The SS Division *Adolf Hitler* – the crack German regiment – was in Dieppe now. The Tiger tanks of the Panzers rolled down the broad boulevards.

Seeking shelter with French families only when they had

to, and at other times crouching low and running through the streets with snipers' bullets snarling around them, Quintain and Marianne worked their way nearer and nearer to the heart of the battle – the mile-long, scimitar-shaped Dieppe waterfront. It took them over an hour.

R.A.F. fighters were already laying smoke over the East headland, and every ship that could be spared was coming in towards the shore, when Quintain and Marianne finally made contact with a patrol of the Canadian Cameron Highlanders. They would be – and were – taken off with the troops who had survived disaster.*

Shells still screamed overhead. Explosions sounded con-

*BEHAVIOUR OF DIEPPE CIVIL POPULATION
SECRET GERMAN FIELD-INTELLIGENCE REPORT
31st Infantry Division   *Hq 24th August 1942*

The civilian population in the divisional sector manifested complete indifference at the scene of the British raid of August 19th, 1942. On the actual scenes of the combat the population was given complete liberty. There have been no reports of sabotage. It has, however, been reported that the population did not disguise its satisfaction at the rapid conclusion of the conflict. Many people displayed some bitterness in declaring that the British had carefully spared their own troops at the expense of non-British forces.

It has been learnt that, in certain cases, the French were specially disposed to the German soldiers engaged in the battle. Thus, an ambulance reported to be French, carrying two French nuns, went to the aid of German wounded soldiers and drove them to the main first aid post. They were at pains to give first aid to the German soldiers. A few of the French, despite enemy fire, gave information about the enemy. In the fighting sectors, the German troops in the line received refreshments and cigarettes from the French inhabitants. One unit reports that reinforcements en route were offered bicycles and motor cycles to reach their destination more rapidly. The Dieppe fire brigade, despite cannon and machine-gun fire from aircraft, unremittingly fought the fires.

The outcome of the battle – the crushing defeat of the enemy – has filled the German troops with confidence and considerably reinforced our defences. During the day of the battle and during the following days the civil population did not conceal its admiration by its behaviour and by its friendly gestures.

The anglophile section of the population, although the prospects of a British attack in force are evidently finished, and despite all outward reservations, has expressed its satisfaction at this event. The German

tinually. Oerlikons thudded. Enemy fighters came out of the smoke which screened the little ships from the shore, and their machine-guns were blazing. Wounded crammed the deck of the little ship which took Quintain and Marianne out to sea. Every available inch of space had its bodies.

The town of Dieppe was a mile away now; a mile back over the tormented, shell-shocked sea. And Quintain and Marianne worked over the wounded together, giving what help they could.

Helping hands were in short supply.

For there were too few doctors, too few trained orderlies, and practically no pain-killing drugs or medical supplies. Four Hospital Landing Craft had been included in the massive flotilla setting out on the raid, but when – at nine o'clock in the morning – it had become plain that the beaches at Dieppe could not be taken, the craft had been turned around and sent back to England again.

So Quintain and Marianne did what they could for the wounded, and around and above them the thunder of war was still loud, but it had begun to recede a little. They looked

---

victory has been accepted unwillingly by these implacable anglophiles. They insist that if the British had not been restrained by their anxiety to spare the civilian population and the town of Dieppe, the latter would rapidly have fallen into their hands.

The purely peasant section of the population remained quiet and absolutely indifferent, solely preoccupied with getting in the harvest. The only emotion shown was at places where their wagons were requisitioned.

After the battle, the civilian population helped to pick up and bury the fallen British, after having been invited to do so by the military authorities.

In two places, French peasants brought in carrier pigeons which had been dropped in cages by parachute. These carrier pigeons bore questionnaires apparently designed to be filled in by civilians before the birds were released.

The division has been ordered by the competent authorities to reward these civilians.

It has also been reported that, at Varengeville, near the battery, some civilians revealed the presence of a British soldier carrying special apparatus. The Feldgendarmerie is checking this information.

up from their work, straightening their backs, and they saw a long line of destroyers, hulls-down to Dieppe, firing round after round into the town, covering the withdrawal. They turned their heads and, on either side of them, other little ships like their own made course for England.*

The little ships which had proved their worth at Dunkirk did so again now.

Closer in towards Dieppe, bodies floated on the water, slackly on the turn of the tide. A seagull, bewildered at finding the sea littered with dead and the sky filled with molten, murderous metal, landed on the deck amid the wounded and refused to leave. A man with one leg blown away forced back the pain in his eyes and offered the gull some broken biscuits. The bird accepted them without fear.

Quintain said to Marianne: "Well, we made it." And he sounded neither sad nor sorry.

She nodded. "Yes."

*Just at the moment that the general withdrawal was ordered, the destroyer HMS *Berkeley* was lost.

Two hundred and fifty years before, on 22nd July 1694, a British admiral called Berkeley had reduced Dieppe to ashes. Anchored a few cables from the town, he had set fire to 3,000 houses with white hot shot. Dieppe was wiped clean off the map, and Berkeley withdrew in triumph.

Now, at 1300 hrs on August 19th, 1942, HMS *Berkeley* was busy in the manner of her illustrious forebear pouring shot and shell into the houses on White beach, when the Luftwaffe pressed home an attack and three Dornier bombers dived down at her.

One, intercepted by British fighters, jettisoned its bombs whilst taking evasive action, and two of these bombs – purely by chance – hit the *Berkeley*. She was immediately blown in two.

Lt. Griffiths, in S.G.B. 8 (steam gunboat) immediately went to the rescue, and picked up all the crew of the destroyer.

Aboard, in addition to her British complement, the *Berkeley* carried American observers, and one of these, a Lt. Colonel Hillsinger, was that day wearing a pair of magnificent new boots of which he was inordinately proud.

One of the bombs which hit the Berkeley blew off one of his feet. He made himself a tourniquet with his tie, then, catching sight of his beautiful new boot floating alongside him with his severed foot still inside it, he tore off his second boot. "Have the bloody pair!" And threw it after the first.

He wiped sweat out of his eyes with the back of a smoke-blackened hand. He said: "Funny thing. I never doubted that I would make it – somehow. But there were times when I had my doubts about you. Even before we got to France, I had my doubts about you."

"What do you mean?"

"Before we arrived in France," Quintain told her, "there were times when I thought *you* might be the traitor of Gourney-en-Bray. There were times when I thought you'd be the one I'd have to shoot."

She stared at him. And then suddenly shivered.

"I'm glad you changed your mind," she said. "I'm glad you didn't make a mistake."

He eyed her appraisingly and the thought that he'd had when he'd first seen her returned.

Despite what they had been through, she was still very attractive.

"I'm glad too," he said, and grinned then.

But there was no time for more talk after that. More talk between them would have to wait.

From here on, until they reached the shores of England again, the wounded needed their undivided attention.

H.M.S. *Calpe* – Headquarters ship – swung around; returned for one last look at the battlefield. At full speed, raked by enemy fire, she steamed along parallel with the beach, but there was nothing to be seen – only the heart-rending wreckage of war, and the mute evidence of defeat.

The flower of Canadian manhood sprawled lifelessly on the blood-soaked stones.

Ripped remnants of tanks dotted the desolate scene. Beyond the West Hill, under high cliffs, the foredoomed Mount Royals were seen crowding the narrow beach, being systematically slaughtered by enemy cross-fire. As the destroyer raced into view round the headland, guns blazing defiance, men leapt to their feet and waved in delirious joy, thinking she was bringing them a deliverance.

But their cheers turned to curses, and they shook their fists after her as she swung away and headed out to the sea.

They were the expendable men – the unlucky Mount Royals. Landed in the wrong place, meat for the butcher right from the start, they were abandoned to their fate.